PRIDE OF MERCIA

PRIDE OF MERCIA

Wallis Peel

CHIVERS

British Library Cataloguing in Publication Data available

This Large Print edition published by BBC Audiobooks Ltd, Bath, 2010.
Published by arrangement with the Author.

U.K. Hardcover ISBN 978 1 408 49191 1
U.K. Softcover   ISBN 978 1 408 49192 8

Printed and bound in Great Britain by
CPI Antony Rowe, Chippenham and Eastbourne

For
Joey and Steve Kingman

654 AD

It is historical fact that Wulfhere, one of the sons of King Penda of Mercia, was taken by three earldormen and hidden for three years. History does not explain where he was taken nor why. Perhaps this story gives a reasonable explanation.

Because of the story, I have used the writer's licence to condense the timescale a little.

It is historical fact that King Penda did die on the banks of the stream called Winwaed at Loidis which is today's Leeds.

CHAPTER ONE

Sihtric reeled in the saddle. The blood oozed in a steady stream, and he wondered just how much longer he had before death snatched him. His great strength had long gone, and he stayed in the saddle through pure balance, plus the drive to get home and tell them.

How far had he come? He shook his head and gritted his teeth to concentrate and calculate. He seemed to have been riding for ever, which was nonsense, but twice he knew he had gone wrong. The forests were so thick in parts, and the trails were not always reliable. The sun was fickle as well, which had not helped a dying man to navigate.

He eased back on the reins and swayed a little, while one hand clutched the wound in his side. The blue tunic had almost been torn from his back and blood welled down his cross-gartered trousers to lodge in his well-cut boots. So much blood! How much could a man lose before he died?

His cloak had failed to withstand the battle, and only his round pin broach remained. It hung loose and threatened to fall. His face was covered with mud and sweat, and was now heavily crinkled with pain lines. He shook his head to clear his mind, and promptly regretted this. He *had* to get back to warn them, and he shuddered. To think he was the only surviving member of the king's gesith.

He had fought well and valiantly, willing to die beside his king but a final, flashing look from King Penda's eyes plus a few shouted words in a direct order had told him what he was expected to do.

King Penda knew he and his Mercians were doomed. It would be a shameful defeat on the banks of the Winwaed stream at Loidis, but King Oswiu and his fierce Northumbrians had been just too much for them.

'Warn my people!' King Penda's eyes had flashed. 'They must prepare a new king!'

Sihtric had not hesitated. He had run for his horse, vaulted onto his saddle, and managed to gallop despite the awful spear wound, which had come at the last second.

He could not help but let his thoughts drift as he allowed his tired horse to walk for a while. Exactly why the battle had taken place in the first place he was not too sure. It was agreed that King Oswiu was the enemy of Mercia but he had not hesitated to let his elder son marry Penda's daughter while Oswiu's younger son was a hostage of Penda. So what had gone wrong? Was it religion, Sihtric asked himself?

King Penda, like Sihtric, followed the true God Woden but King Penda had always been a tolerant man. He had allowed the strange, robed and hooded men to come down from

2

Northumbria and relate their ridiculous story of someone, in another distant land, who had died nailed to two pieces of wood.

Was it possible that King Penda's laxity upon religious matters had offended Woden? Perhaps everyone had been lax with their prayers and sacrifices. Sihtric shook his head slowly. Whatever it might be that had brought this disaster down upon Mercia, he would have no further part in its well-being. He could smell death upon himself.

His life had been good, with three wives, which was not unnatural when so many died giving birth. Of his many children only two had managed to survive to adulthood, but they were fine, strong and healthy. He frowned for a minute. Elfrida, his daughter, was fifteen years old now and she should have been married at least a year ago. The trouble was, Elfrida was stubborn, with a mind of her own and perfectly well prepared to argue the toss even with him.

Now his son Cynewulf, a year younger than his sister, was another matter. It was true, he was well trained with all weapons, but Cynewulf was—and Sihtric hunted for the correct word—his son was not terribly bright and he had reservations about him.

On more than one occasion it was Elfrida who had beaten her brother in their childish fights, which was, surely, all wrong? She could be so aggressive and dominant, and Cynewulf

3

definitely had a hesitant streak in his makeup, which bothered Sihtric. Surely a son of his could be neither soft, nor cowardly?

His horse stumbled and jolted him. He could not help let out a grunt at the pain. He held the reins more firmly, heeled his mount and collected it up again. He eyed the sky; not long past noon so, with luck, surely he could get back home before night?

He started to daydream again, not so much because of tiredness or carelessness, but more from that mystical state that heralds death—when the borderline between living and dying is just a thread.

At thirty-nine years old, he had done very well for himself because he owned twenty hides of very good land, which was valued at just over twelve hundred shillings, which made him a Twelfhyde man. His cattle and pigs thrived on this land, although it was a constant battle to stop the forest invading again. He had plenty of cottars and gerbers in his power. The former worked for him every Monday, as well as extra days at harvest time. The gerbers paid their dues in money and produce as well as by their labour. He had never bothered to hold slaves, because they could be a poor crop to raise. Even the best, well-trained slave only equalled eight oxen in value. Slaves could also be a nuisance.

Was Cynewulf capable of handling his estate? Sihtric bit his lip doubtfully. Elfrida certainly was but he wished for no trouble between brother and sister. Even nowadays there were times when they quarrelled, far more than siblings should.

Two years ago, in a miserable winter, a lord's travelling clerk had arrived and Sihtric had had his Will drawn up. He could neither read nor write himself because runic letters were hard to learn as well as form. Not that this mattered. His Will had been read to him and checked by an elder, and he knew the Witan would see his wishes were carried out with scrupulous fairness. When Elfrida did finally decide upon a young man she would take him a first-rate dower.

He made himself sit up straight again and take notice of where he was because he knew he could not stay in this saddle for much longer. Was there a familiarity about this area? And his hope soared. He watched his horse's ears prick; the animal knew where he was and started to quicken his pace.

Sihtric winced and groaned as the horse broke into a canter, oblivious to the bit now. The animal scented fires, human scents and odours from domesticated animals including its own old companions.

"Hang on!" Sihtric grunted to himself. "Don't give up now when you are so near!" he self-rebuked but oh, what an effort it all was.

* * *

Elfrida preened herself as she hung over the pool. A careful study of each feature showed, although no great beauty, she was not to be ignored either, where looks were concerned. She had a nice high forehead, a smart little nose, topped with deep blue eyes. Her hair was fine and flaxen and her lips, not too ripe, and certainly not for pouting, were meant to be kissed—so why didn't he?

Because he did not know she existed, she told herself a little petulantly and gave a huge sigh. How stupid boys could be at times. She sat up straight and removed an imaginary crease from her tunic, whose colour matched her eyes. Elfrida knew she was very fashion-conscious, not that it seemed to do much good with him. Her trousers were a light tan, brown the same colour as her belt, to which was attached her long, bladed, exceedingly sharp dagger.

Her thoughts came back to Wulfhere again. Where was he now? She had hunted for him, without success, then given it up as a bad job. When Wulfhere took it into his head to vanish he did just that. Surely he was not with Osburga once more? She bit her lip with worry. Osburga was as dark as she was fair, and she had a pair of eyes almost black in colour. What did Osburga have that she did not? It was too infuriating for words.

From this position she was partially hidden,

but could still see the tun. To one side stood the flimsy homes which were built over a pit in the ground. Elfrida, as one of the nobility, lived in a better house constructed of wattle and daub, which had a wooden floor. Their house was almost waterproof, except in the most bitter storms, and it was reasonably comfortable, though the winds in the winter found every nook and cranny.

Her thoughts switched to her brother. Deep down, she did not really like him, but with Father away so much they were thrown together more than she really cared for. Cynewulf was—she pondered over him—her brother was not as hard as he should be. She was a firstborn, but, as the girl, he was inclined to look down upon her, which usually resulted in Elfrida smacking him on the end of his tender nose, then dancing out of his reach. Because Cynewulf lumbered. He had no grace at all. It was true that he was well made, with height, and the promise of great muscles when fully grown but he was so slow that he sent a message before using his hands or weapons.

Elfrida knew she could run rings around him, because, although tall for a girl, she was wiry and swift. When she made a comparison between her brother and where her heart lay, she always ended up shaking her head. It was true, Wulfhere did not have the best of temperaments. He could be moody, arrogant, hot-tempered and just a little too quick to use

7

his royal position for his own advantage.

That did not matter. Elfrida, with a wisdom beyond her years, knew that, as males matured, many came to be more reasonable and who was better to be the wife of the king's son than herself? She was fully trained in all weapons; a skilled tracker; a good hunter and beautifully educated. She could read and write and knew all their laws and customs. She understood domestic matters and estate management. Her breeding was impeccable.

She thought about her beloved father. She knew she was his favourite without realising this was because she was a mirror of her long-dead mother. Elfrida also suspected that her father was uncertain about his only son, who was a constant, deep worry to him. Poor Cynewulf, she grinned. If he was not in trouble from one direction then it was from another. If only he would stop and think things through instead of stamping around like a young bull, scenting his first cow on heat.

She knew that, reluctantly, she must head back to the tun centre. Her tunic rippled with her movements. It was made from fine linen, skilfully woven by slaves and was worth many sceats, though she had never handled a coin so far. There was no need, because when Father was away, as now, the Witan oversaw the needs of brother and sister. She had been carefully taught the value of money; the sceat, penig and styca. A pound was a very rare coin and no one here had ever seen one.

Alicia watched her pass and sniffed. She did not really care for Elfrida, but she did like her brother so went out of her way to try and be friendly. She tossed her brown hair, and eyed Elfrida enviously. What splendid clothing, and that expensive brooch! Alicia wallowed in a wave of hot jealousy.

'Have you been walking far?' she asked quietly, falling into step.

Elfrida threw her a look. Now, what did she want? She knew Alicia was besotted with her brother and thought she was mad. She shrugged: 'Why?'

Alicia had the grace to blush and drop her eyes. Elfrida was stuck up just because of her breeding. She stifled the hot retort, which rose to her lips though. It would be most improvident to antagonise Elfrida, who was quite capable of punching her face. 'Just wondered,' she mumbled and knew she had gone scarlet.

Elfrida saw through her and wondered why she felt a flash of pity for Alicia. She was certainly of Cynewulf's calibre, short on brains, but long on ambition, and would it do either of them any good?

She spotted Cynewulf from her eye corner, and drew Alicia's attention to him, while watching her face. Suddenly, she felt a rare flash of empathy for Alicia. It was so obvious to her that Alicia thought the sun and moon shone on Cynewulf, who appeared not to know she existed. This meant the girl was in the same exasperating position as herself for Wulfhere. 'They are infuriating at times, aren't they?' she said in a quiet, confidential voice.

Alicia was startled, then she saw pity and understanding in Elfrida's eyes. Her interest flared. Did that mean she had her eyes fixed on someone too? 'Maddeningly so!' she replied. 'And here comes your brother now!'

Elfrida groaned inwardly. If Cynewulf was in one of his tormenting moods she knew she would go for him, because her heartache was suddenly resolved. How blind and stupid she had been. As Wulfhere was one of King Penda's sons, all she had to do was ask her father to speak for her!

'I'm going!' Alicia said, hoping Cynewulf would chase after her. He was so handsome. He made her thighs go all weak and trembling.

'Well, Sister!' Cynewulf stated, halting before her, oblivious to Alicia's departure. 'Why so serious?'

'Where have you been?' Elfrida demanded.

Cynewulf gave a shrug which could have meant anything. 'Here and there.'

'What about your studying?' she asked practically. Even though there were days when she disliked her brother she was conscious of her additional two years.

Cynewulf grimaced. He was nearly a replica of his sister, except his eyes were grey, and his

10

hair much darker. He was thickset, and perhaps even a little too fat for someone so young, because Cynewulf adored his food. 'Writing is for clerks, not warriors!' he said with a grin.

Elfrida shook her head. She knew he hated studying for the simple reason it was such hard work to him. He was a poor scholar, and how he would manage an estate one day was beyond her. If he married Alicia, would she prove capable? This was a new thought, and she was uncertain whether she liked it. Then her eyes opened wide. 'Don't turn around!' she hissed at Cynewulf. 'Just walk off quietly with me. We can run when we're round the corner!'

Cynewulf went stiff and tightened the grip on his spear but obeyed. Elfrida was nobody's fool. 'Who is it?'

'Lord Burhred!'

Cynewulf paled. Burhred was the senior elder with a testy temper, and no patience at all for the young. He was highly respected, heading the Witan in the king's absence, and everyone hung on his every word.

They rounded a corner and broke into a mad run, bolting for the fringe of the forest. Inside the trees they stopped and looked back apprehensively. 'Did he see us?' Cynewulf asked nervously, quite terrified of this elder.

Elfrida pulled a face. 'Since when did he ever miss anything?'

Cynewulf groaned. 'I messed up my lessons,

11

and he beat me and I can't help it,' he complained bitterly. 'I'm not clever at things like you. Anyhow, why should I bother to learn? I can always engage a clerk. Father cannot read or write, and it's not harmed him!'

Elfrida knew when not to argue. Cynewulf's face held a pout, and he was halfway into one of his famous sulks. If Alicia could see him now, she told herself, she might have a few reservations, but she held her tongue. In one way, she felt pity for her brother, because at times he was pathetic.

Cynewulf looked back through the trees, his shoulders slumped a little. Then he flashed a look at his sister. He would never admit it, but there were times when she scared the living daylights out of him. She was so good at whatever she did . . . it simply was unfair. Then he brightened and turned back to her. 'I know something you don't know!' he hissed, his voice edged with triumph.

Elfrida held her breath. One of Cynewulf's more unpleasant traits was his ability to gossip like an old woman who had nothing better to do. 'What is it?' she asked wearily. Some ridiculous tittle-tattle.

'It's about Wulfhere!' he told her and grinned. He did not like the king's middle son, for the simple reason he was scared of him. There were times when Wulfhere resembled a bad-tempered bear just out of hibernation. 'He's in love!' he chuckled. 'And smitten with it!'

Elfrida felt a cold hand squeeze her heart, but willed her features to remain impassive. She broke eye contact to remove an imaginary speck of dirt from her tunic. 'Who?' she asked nonchalantly.

'It's Osburga!' Cynewulf confided and waited, watching her sharply.

Elfrida was a superb actress, though it was a struggle to cover up her emotions. 'So?' she drawled, noncommittally, while her heart hammered. It could not be true, could it? Was that why he ignored her?

Cynewulf suddenly stiffened: 'Something has happened. People are shouting! There's a rider just come in, and . . . Oh! People are running. Come on, it may be news of Father!'

They both raced back the way they had come, and rather rudely pushed themselves through the milling crowd as a rider fell from his horse. Then Elfrida used her elbows ruthlessly and pushed her way to the front.

'Father!' she cried in horror and fell down on her knees beside him. Cynewulf stood a pace behind, not yet able to take in and believe the scene before his eyes.

'Get back all of you!' a stentorian voice bellowed, and Burhred ruthlessly hurled people aside with the rest of the Witan at his heels.

Sihtric looked up as his senses began to swim. He had done it, but at what cost? He

13

heard the people and thought he recognised individual voices. 'Elfrida?' he croaked uncertainly.

'Yes! I'm here!' she cried.

'I too, my lord!' Burhred announced and frowned. This man was very near to death indeed. From the state of his dress he knew there could not be much blood left in his body so he forced his creaking knees to bend and kneel, with his head to the other warrior. 'Your news?' he asked anxiously.

Sihtric struggled to assemble coherent speech. 'We have lost the battle, and King Penda will be dead by now. Northumbria rules, and shortly their men will be down here. You are to pick a new king, I was ordered to tell you!' he blurted out with the last dregs of its strength.

Burhred was appalled. Elfrida felt the tears streaming down her cheeks because she loved her father dearly. Cynewulf stood flat-footed and disbelieving.

Elfrida took her father's limp hand into hers. The skin was so white. Yet this side of his body was red and sticky. Cynewulf had no words but he felt a strange prickle at the back of his eyes. Between himself and his father there had been a barrier that he had never understood. His father could not just die and leave them.

Burhred was thinking rapidly. It was unlikely the Northumbrians were on their way down here right now. They would be too busy celebrating. So how much time could he count on? He eyed the dying man. A few more minutes and that will be it, he told himself. It was staggering that he had been able to ride from Loidis in this state but, then, that was his breeding. His daughter came from the same vital metal; it was a pity her brother did not.

'We lost badly, my lord?' he asked heavily.

Sihtric looked at him. 'Very badly,' he croaked, and his eyes flashed what he could not say. It had been slaughter. The pride of Mercia was no more. Then he forced himself to practical matters. 'My Will! I charge you to see to my Will. Elfrida, you are told, and you too, son. Obey the elders. Why has it gone so dark? I thought it was still afternoon!' he gasped, speech now too much of an effort. He slitted his eyes for a final look at his beloved daughter, managed one meaningful glance at Burhred and died. Bled to death.

As Elfrida let herself go so Cynewulf felt free to indulge in his own tears of shock, while he stood miserably. The siblings' world had collapsed. What was their life going to be like under the thumb of the elders, especially Lord Burhred?

Burhred stepped back, turned and strode away. This had always been an outside possibility, although he had not expected it quite so soon. How could the pride of Mercia be so trampled on the banks of the Winwaed stream at that barbaric place called Loidis? It just did not make sense. Yet it had happened.

CHAPTER TWO

Burhred marched through the tun, seemingly indifferent to it, yet acutely aware of who was where and why. In his opinion, it was a good place to live, because it was quite large and contained over five hundred households. The palace stood on the left, and he eyed it thoughtfully and gave a tiny shake to his head. Somehow, their four classes of rank annoyed him. The best was, in his opinion, that of the churl while he, as a dignified, respected and powerful earldorman, received nothing but trouble and problems for his rank.

He spotted a movement and halted, eyes narrow, and beckoned. The young man stepped into view, his fishing rod in one hand and a spear in the other. There was no doubt he was a handsome youth, and, when fully developed and grown, would make an outstanding man, but now he constantly annoyed Burhred. He still had a youth's lanky body with under-developed muscles, and his eyes, too often, wore either arrogance or a fit of the sulks. King Penda's middle son left much to be desired though, deep down, Burhred liked him, but no one had the faintest idea, certainly not Wulfhere.

'Your father, the king, is dead!' he barked unceremoniously. 'Get over there, then return to where you were fishing. I'll want to see you. Move, I say! Now, not tomorrow!'

'Dead?' Wulfhere gasped, hardly able to believe his ears. He could not move and gave a tiny shake to his head. This was news that had never entered his mind. His great father, like King Pybba before him, had an air; an aura of regality, which commanded instant respect and Wulfhere was well aware he lacked this. No matter what he did, people sniggered at him behind his back. To counter his deep hurt, he swaggered, not realising he was simply compounding youthful faults. How could his father be dead? It was impossible for such a brave, skilled warrior. He gulped, struggling to assimilate the shock, aware that the dreaded Burhred held him in his iron gaze.

'Now!' Burhred thundered.

Wulfhere jumped forward. No one in their right mind argued the toss with this lord who had been such a brilliant fighter in his younger days, alongside Mercia's old King Pybba. He took to his heels, still stunned and wished desperately there was someone with whom he could talk sincerely.

Then the full implication hit him. Mercia was kingless! A state of affairs that would have to be remedied forthwith and he was one of Penda's sons. A sharp doubt hit him. Elder

17

brother Peada? He scowled at the very thought. He was a married man, and logically next in line, but Wulfhere gritted his teeth. He loathed brother Peada and suspected this feeling was returned in full.

Burhred watched his retreating back and knew his thoughts to the last syllable. He sniffed, then gave a surreptitious look around before grunting with approval. They were following him, coming from different directions, strolling as if they did not have a care in the world. Good, he muttered to himself. Now to find somewhere very private and discreet, and he knew exactly where to go. It was true, the three of them if seen together would make tongues work fast and in one direction only but this could not be helped under these horrific circumstances.

With an agility surprising in a man who had reached the remarkable age of fifty-five years, he scrambled through some bushes onto a small animal trail and strode briskly. He halted in a little clearing and heard the others following, making too much noise of course, and he shook his head. He was not impatient, it gave him time to reorganise his shocked thoughts. So when they reached him he stood calm and seemingly unperturbed.

They looked at him. He really was remarkable. Even though his hair had thinned and started to frost he was still a fine figure of a man: upright, bold and very dangerous when crossed. He was tall, with wide shoulders, and his muscles, although not as hard as they had once been, were still well formed with strength.

He studied them in turn. Eanwulf was forty years old and showed it with his bowed shoulders, and a shortness of breath. He was smaller than Burhred, built more on square, stocky lines. Ealstan, one year younger, had worn better, with his thin, lighter frame, but he limped from an old leg wound and already his joints had started to stiffen and cripple.

Burhred eyed them. Where he led, they would follow, which was one great plus point—Eanwulf without hesitation; Ealstan after he had worried and grumbled at real and imaginary obstacles.

'I never expected this!' Eanwulf stated flatly.

'What a fool thing to think!' Burhred told himself. Men always died in battles and kings were certainly not exempt. 'So?' he grunted, which could have meant anything.

Ealstan was the more practical of two. 'What do we do first?'

This was more like it and Burhred nodded approvingly. 'First we have to find our king and bury him, if we can. Secondly, we will now review our options. Thirdly, we will discuss whom the next is to be. After that, it will be a case of any other matters. Questions?' he asked them in his usual gruff manner.

Ealstan spoke first: 'I've already sent some

men off to try and find the king's body so that is number one out of the way.'

Burhred was pleased. There were times when Ealstan surprised him with flashes of initiative. The pity was this did not happen often enough.

Burhred shook his head. 'We are in pretty bad shape.' He confirmed what his companions had already suspected. 'We have lost over half of our fighting men and of the remainder many will be wounded, struggling to make their way back here. Our position is very bad!' he said dourly.

'We do have the women!' Eanwulf reminded him.

Burhred, flashed him a sharp look. 'If we lose them as well in battle we shall die out as a race. No breeding!'

Ealstan had another more pressing worry. 'Do you think the Northumbrians will invade us right away?'

Burhred shook his head. This was a question that had occupied him for some deep thought until he had worked it out logically. 'They won't come as invaders. Their King Oswiu won't have that. Apart from celebrating their victory, they too will have wounded to get home. What I suspect is emissaries will be sent very shortly to exact tribute from us. We may have one week in the clear, but no more!'

Ealstan grunted. 'We must strip the tun of our wealth. Hide everything. Remove the best breeding stock and—!'

Eanwulf shook his head. 'How do you propose to do that with Peada around?' he asked sourly. 'He's not blind!'

'Exactly!' Burhred snapped. 'We may have to be prepared to lose half of our wealth in monies. I buried my own when all the men went to war,' he told them a little smugly. 'You two should have done the same!'

Ealstan was stung. 'I did not think it would be necessary!' he retorted.

Burhred gave him a cold look, then turned to the main matter. 'The Witan has to pick a new king and before the Northumbrians get here as well,' he told them heavily.

Eanwulf gave him a harsh look. 'You don't mean—?'

Ealstan finish the sentence for him. 'Peada?'

Burhred grimaced and shrugged his shoulders. 'Who else will they pick? We three have our own opinions, which will not match those of the others. When it comes down to a vote, we will get nowhere. Anyhow, the time is not right. So we must lie low. We will simply abstain,' he told them firmly.

They looked at each other. So who was going to voice the name first? Burhred did it for them. 'Of course Wulfhere is the best son at the moment, at least until we see how Aethelred turns out, but that will be years away. It is the here and now which concerns us.'

Eanwulf shook his head. 'It wouldn't even be wise to mention Wulfhere's name because he is so despised for his general unpleasant attitude.'

Ealstan pulled a face. 'The stupid boy! He has the right make and shape to be a king but I have grave reservations whether he will ever be fit for that the position. He is nothing but a bad-tempered, spoiled, detestable brat, who wants knocking from here, right up to Northumbria and back again!'

Burhred concurred. The description was one he could not have bettered. 'Peada is twenty years now, a married man, and settled. Aethelred is only nine with Wulfhere in between, so Peada it is sure to be.'

Eanwulf demurred. 'Someone could challenge to be king by the right of battle,' he reminded them quickly. The son of a king did not necessarily take this position just by right of birth. He must have proven qualities, which involved brains as well as muscles.

Burhred's mind raced over possibilities and probabilities, then he shook his head firmly. All other possible contenders had died with their king, on the banks of the Winwaed stream at Loidis. Those few who did survive would lack the basic qualifications. 'Wulfhere is the best man for Mercia but I know they will pick Peada!' he said angrily.

Eanwulf agreed. 'He will be useless. He is nothing but a dreamer. All his talk of poetry and rhyming with couplets, but he will be Oswiu's man, that's for sure,' he stated, and gave a sigh.

Ealstan agreed. 'Peada is too womanish. Say what you like about Wulfhere, he is all-male!'

Eanwulf pointed out something else. 'He is also in love, which will make him even more impossible to handle.'

Burhred groaned. Why had he not known of this before? Was he slipping? 'Who is it?' he asked wearily.

'He can't marry her anyhow,' Eanwulf continued thoughtfully.

Burhred's eyes narrowed. 'Why? Is she betrothed to someone else?'

Eanwulf shook his head. 'He's too closely related,' he told them.

Their marriage laws were very strict for the good and unity of them as a whole. Inbreeding only weakened the stock and was something to be abhorred.

'Who?' Burhred barked. As if he did not have enough problems without something like this.

Eanwulf told him, 'Osburga, daughter of Sebright, son of—!'

'Spare me her pedigree. I know it!' Burhred snapped, getting angry now. Had Wulfhere gone quite stupid? 'Of course he can't marry her. He's not fit to marry anyone at the moment. Get rid of her and quickly. Arrange for her betrothal with someone faraway!'

Ealstan saw a problem. 'She might object!'

Burhred's temper rose very high. It was true, no maid could be forced to marry against her will but the future of the tribe came before any girl's temperamental objections. 'She obeys me on this or I'll take her hide off,' he grated and his companions knew he meant it. 'Make her dower very large indeed and also give her some land. She can always exchange it for hides of land elsewhere, but get her out of this tun before dawn!' he bellowed.

Ealstan started to grin and Eanwulf had to join in. Burhred in a rage was a sight to behold. No wonder he could terrify so many others but they knew him too well. Also, more to the point, they were his only sworn and trustworthy allies. Without them, he was powerless as a lone individual.

'What's Wulfhere going to say when he finds out, and who is going to tell him?' Eanwulf asked.

Burhred sniffed. 'I will, and a few other home truths as well!' Then his mind moved on to more important matters. 'Oswiu will want Peada as king. Don't forget, if we had another such defeat we would cease to exist as a tribe, except as slaves. A final point, if Wulfhere stays around here someone might just put a knife in his back. So—we will hide him until the time is ripe for him to challenge to be king. And don't ask me where just now. I want to think on it tonight. I have an idea, but I will have to consult someone and complicated arrangements will have to be made before my plan can be bought to fruition.'

'Hide him—where?' Ealstan challenged.

'Not in Mercia, that's for sure. He has to go where he is totally unknown, and I have the very place in mind, and the right companion for him as well!'

Eanwulf eyed him. Burhred was the most cunning and devious man he had ever known, and, deep down, he was thankful they were both on the same side. He knew this view was shared by Ealstan. Burhred had no scruples at all where Mercia was concerned. He could be an exceedingly dangerous man. At the same time, he needed to take his own precautions because he was so feared.

Burhred read his mind and a sardonic grin crossed his face. 'I am very careful. I take great precautions, and my slave tastes all my food before I do. I have a shadow at my back most of the time, who is as good as a reliable hound!'

His companions nodded with satisfaction. 'Where?'

'Down with the Hwicce!' Burhred told them triumphantly.

His companions were startled then started to grin. 'At Glevum?' Ealstan asked.

The Hwicce were a large tribe of seven thousand households scattered over the wide Severn Valley region, as well as most of the

25

hilly area. They paid tribute to Mercia and, deep down, all Mercians despised them for this. They were a tribe of mixed Saxon and Angle stock with a heavy dash of the old British, as well as Romano. They came down from the Dubonii tribe. Many decades ago, they had been fine fighters, especially when it came to guerrilla tactics, but over the decades they had suffered too many defeats. For as long as could be remembered the Hwicce had been content to pay tribute to the King of Mercia, who had become their overlord. Marriage and social intercourse between Hwicce and Mercia was permitted, unmarred by friction, but the Mercians still retained their ability to look down their noses at all of the Hwicce people.

Eanwulf eyed Burhred. 'Can they be trusted?' he asked softly.

Burhred let out a snort. 'Of course they can't! Would you trust any tribe who lived in subjugation? Don't forget also *we* are now going to be doomed to pay our tribute to Northumbria. Do you think they will trust us? Like hell they will! They will infiltrate us with spies just to see what we're getting up to.'

Ealstan nodded glumly. 'That's true!'

Eanwulf felt he had to argue this point. 'We are the greater tribe, and can muster over 12,000 households, and—!'

'No warriors left to fight!' Burhred pointed out impatiently. 'Use your brains!'

Eanwulf glowered at him, then decided it was more prudent to shut up. Burhred was getting into one of his bad-tempered moods. 'So what do you plan?' he hurled at him.

Burhred hastened to explain. Eanwulf's face wore a mulish look and Ealstan's lips were tight. 'Glevum is no good, Wulfhere would get a knife in his back as quick as staying here, because you can bet Northumbria will send spies down that far. I plan for him to go to a small unknown place, and vanish for two or even three years. He will be trained there in everything, then, when we judge the time right, we fetch him back and he challenges for the kingship.'

His companions considered. They hunted backwards and forwards for flaws. 'Where exactly?'

'At a little place, known as Gete. It only has a handful of households at the best of times. It is on the bank of a little river called the Frome and tribute is paid by a very insignificant lord. I found it quite by chance many years ago when exploring and hunting. I filed it away in my memory for just such an eventuality as this!'

'What's so special about it?' Ealstan asked.

Burhred's eyes glowed with triumph. 'That's the whole point! There is nothing special to attract anyone's attention. It's humdrum, ugly, useless, with land neither high nor low. The so-called river is more of a stream, except when it goes in spate after a wet winter. The hunting is very good, because people are so scarce. It's quiet and peaceful, so our young hothead should be able to keep himself out of trouble for a while—especially with the companion I'm going to send!' and his eyes gleamed wolfishly, while he explained a little further.

'What about the Lord there?'

Burhred eyed him wickedly. 'He only has seven hides of land, so really is a nobody. I'll see he gives no trouble and keeps his mouth shut too. Oddly enough, last year I had inquiries made—my contingency plan!' he said, a little smugly. 'This lord has not done too well breeding a family. He only has one small son and tomorrow I'll see that son is taken hostage and removed elsewhere. One wrong word or deed from that minor lord and he'll only get his son back as a body!'

His companions agreed without hesitation. Harsh situations called for harsh measures, then something occurred to Eanwulf. 'What if Wulfhere refuses to go?'

'He will do as he is told and go, even if it is with a noose around him, and dragged behind a horse. You know the companion I've chosen, and his calibre. Wulfhere will also go and live as a churl, which won't do him any harm either. Get rid of some of his inflated ideas. You know, King Penda did not think all that much of his eldest son. He too thought

28

Wulfhere the best bet and agreed with me some harsh discipline was needed to sort him out. This would be taking place even if King Penda had lived. All we are doing is following a Royal command!'

Burhred eyed them then spoke once more. 'The only person who will know about this arrangement is my good servant Oswald. I will obviously need someone extra to liaise down there and I have my eyes on the perfect person. Now we must all get back, but re-enter the tun each of us alone, and from now on with very tight lips!'

CHAPTER THREE

A thin shaft of sunlight trickled over his body as the clouds danced across the sky and Wulfhere looked upwards. There was little wind; just a tiny breeze, only enough to make the grass and leaves give a minute tremble.

He wore his usual fine garments, as befitted his rank: a good red tunic edged with a paler stripe and dark brown trousers with boots to match. His fine hair, alert eyes, generous mouth and good-looking face were marred, right now, with his emotions.

His eyes were narrow blue chips, while his lips were set in a thin, uncompromising grimace. He felt like bawling his eyes out except men of his age did not cry. He still found it hard to take in. His much adored father was not going to come back, which was impossible. Penda had always been there, available to ruffle his hair and slap him on the back—something never shared with his elder brother, though tough young kid brother Aethelred did not miss out either. Wulfhere felt he had been his father's favourite, which warmed yet also chilled his heart because exactly where did Penda's death leave him? He had begun to learn something about realism, and did not like it one bit.

He was honest enough to know he was thoroughly disliked, no matter what he did. This hurt, because his years were too few for him to have developed a thick skin. Brother Peada was the opposite. He was held in great favour, because he was so good! Peada did not collect enemies; he never lost his temper, nor raised his voice. He was such a disgusting paragon, in Wulfhere's eyes, he was almost unfit to live. Peada would debate with multiple words, and would not dream of resorting to violence. It was not that his elder brother was a coward, no Mercian could be that, Wulfhere told himself, it was simply Peada refused to dirty his elegant hands, which were so expert at writing.

Where was Lord Burhred? Wulfhere wanted to go back home, but it never occurred to him to disobey this lord's orders. Only a few months ago, his father had talked to him about Burhred, extolling his virtues, his wisdom, his loyalty and above all his cunning. At the end of his homily Penda had said strong words to his middle son: 'Do as he tells you always. Don't argue the toss or question in any way. He was the finest warrior Mercia has ever had and he has the finest brain here among us. You can always count on him!'

Wulfhere had been startled at this unusual advice yet, thinking back, there had been so many times in the past when Penda had been closeted with Lord Burhred to the exclusion of all others.

His thoughts switched to Osburga with her glittering dark eyes and lovely figure. He adored her, and his wild heart softened as he made up his mind. Once he was over mourning for his father he would ask someone to speak for him. Marriage came in two parts and the first section was the Pledge when he would offer his gift and state his intentions. The morning after the actual marriage, after consummation, he would donate his Morning Gift, which always became the wife's personal property. The best gift was always land, and his heart swelled as he considered how generous he would be. When he gave the deeds to her would be the time to give his oath.

Like all of his race, divorce was a sad, but understandable necessity at times, which was why the Morning Gift's value was esteemed. At a divorce the female always had this to fall back on as well as half of her husband's estate and effects, which was a sensible way to go about matters. Not that Wulfhere believed there would ever be a divorce, because life with Osburga would be glorious.

He sat so still deeply immersed in these thoughts that the first sound barely registered, then he whipped into alert action. He grasped his bow and ducked behind a nearby thicket as he strained his ears. That was a horse coming at a walk, and he guessed who this had to be but prudently nocked an arrow to his bow.

Burhred rolled into sight, halted his horse and dismounted, grimacing at some knee stiffness. Wulfhere leaped forward to offer polite help, but the testy elder, with a sniff, ignored this. Burhred now hated long rides, but this one was his own fault. Long ago, he had used this spot himself when he wished to commune quite alone, with tangled thoughts, and he had shown it to Wulfhere on one of their rare rides together.

Burhred looked around, then threw a hard look at the young man. Wulfhere hastily remembered his manners, and put his cloak over a nearby log to make a more comfortable seat. He had some cold meat from a young fawn he had killed the day before. It had roasted nicely and was tender, so he slashed up a generous portion, placed it neatly on a large leaf and offered it to his senior.

Burhred grunted, took it and began to eat with fastidious, good manners, eyeing his companion as he did so. He could see Wulfhere was tense and coiled like a snake but he was pleased to note his tongue was held in restraint.

When he had eaten Wulfhere offered a flask of spring water, and Burhred drank slowly, taking his time, wondering which was the best way to start. He decided the beginning was the obvious place.

'The men have returned from the Winwaed stream—without your father's body. It was in full spate and many bodies were carried away, and probably are at sea now.'

Wulfhere was shocked. 'What do we do?' he asked with a catch in his voice. He had managed to stamp his emotion deep into his heart yet this sudden mention of Penda's death pushed prickles to the back of his eyes again.

'We'll have a funeral without the body and make an appropriate sacrifice to Woden, of course!' Burhred growled at him. He was aware he was on the verge of a very bad temper, because there were so many problems hitting him from too many directions. He was also bothered with the final details of his plan and how Wulfhere would react.

He glared at the young man, reinforcing his strong, harsh personality upon the youth and it was Wulfhere who broke eye contact first as a shiver went down his spine.

'The Witan are getting ready to pick the new king and you don't stand a snowball in hell's chance either!' Burhred told him bluntly. He wanted to get this out of the way immediately. 'It will be Peada!'

Wulfhere grimaced. It was only what he had suspected deep in his heart but he could not submit to this tamely. 'Anyone can fight him for the position, especially a brother!' he said forcefully.

Burhred muttered a curse to himself. This was a typical and expected reaction. 'Don't talk wet, boy!' he snapped. 'Because that's what you are. You are still a boy and he is a man. He would make mincemeat of you.'

Wulfhere held his eyes, curbing his temper. 'Perhaps not, and I do have the right to, sir!'

Burhred eyed him thoughtfully. 'So all right, you thrash him and then what? The Witan will still vote against you because you are disliked, and it's your own fault too! You are still far too wet behind the ears. Just because you can handle a few weapons doesn't make you a fighting man. Far from it!'

Wulfhere scowled. 'I don't like this kind of talk!' he grumbled as hotly as he dared.

'Tough!' Burhred shot back quickly. 'You are going to hear a lot more like that before I leave here. You won't like any of it, but you have to put up with it: and wipe that sulky expression from your face, unless you'd like me to backhand you?'

Wulfhere lowered his eyes as resentment boiled in his heart. Burhred would hit him and he muttered to himself, with frustration, but forced himself to sit still and keep his mouth shut.

'What kind of king will Peada make?' he grumbled aloud. 'We'll end up licking the boots of Northumbria before he is finished. He won't fight. I would. I am the better man! I know it!' he dared to say hotly and looked deep into Burhred's cool eyes.

The elder let a smile touch his lips. 'I agree,' he said quietly, defusing the other's temper instantly.

Wulfhere was startled. 'You do? Well arrange for me to be king!' he argued.

Burhred shook his head. 'Not yet, but I will in time, if you can manage to do as I tell you. There is more to being a king than might and strength. Guile and brains are also required and a hefty dose of popularity. Your brother has already volunteered to pay Oswiu's tribute without trouble, and we have to agree. There is nothing else we could do when we have been bled white. We have to re-coup our fighting strength and that is going to take considerable time. Do you think I like the idea of Northumbrians being our masters with King Oswiu as our overlord? Of course I don't! I hate it!' he spat, allowing his emotions to show for a few seconds.

Wulfhere bottled his surprise and eyed him afresh. 'How many others think like you, sir?' he asked in a quiet voice. Perhaps there was hope for him after all.

Burhred settled back into a more comfortable position. His backside must be getting thin or this log was especially knobbly! 'Two only,' he replied shortly. 'Eanwulf and Ealstan. That's all at the moment and there is no chance of fresh allies as things stand at present.'

Wulfhere flinched. He had not realised matters were quite so bad, and he bit his lip with worry. 'My brother is too—womanish!' he managed to get out in disgust.

'Correct!' Burhred concurred, 'so in the future we will do something about it and I empathise the words *in the future*!' he warned with a growl. 'You have to go away for two or even three years!'

Wulfhere doubted his ears. He was appalled. 'What! Where? Why?'

Burhred took time to frame his reply neatly. 'First, we let all this die a natural death,' and he winced at his unfortunate words, before continuing. 'Secondly, to change you from a boy into a real man. No, don't you glower at me like that, you puppy! You think you know it all, yet you are totally ignorant. Initially King Peada will have a very strong following but give it time, and he will hang himself. When he does, I bring you back and make you king but not before. We have to buy time to recoup, train fresh fighters, gather strength again so that when we do go into battle against King Oswiu we will win hands down. We cannot afford a second defeat. In this waiting time, you will vanish and you'll go with a man I've picked, and he will train you, make you work so hard you'll cry quits, but he will make a man of you. He will also make you kingly material, which right now, you are not!'

Wulfhere sat speechless with horror. 'How can I run?' he managed to get out scornfully.

'You won't be running. You will be well and truly dead. I will arrange this. A wild animal will have killed you. You hang around here, and it's quite possible someone will shove a knife between your shoulder blades and where will Mercia be then? It might also invite the killing of young Aethelred as well! If you want to be king you will do exactly as I say. Or I wash my hands of you and turn elsewhere,' he said coldly.

Wulfhere could hardly believe what he was hearing. 'Am I so hated then?' he managed to get out wistfully.

Burhred gave it him straight again. 'Very much so, and it's your own fault for being so cocky and arrogant. Look at you!' and he pointed. 'You call those muscles? Why an infant has better!' he said and flexed his arm to show bulging biceps. 'These have been in a real battle. You don't know what one is. Then there is a matter of your brain. What do you know about handling men, so they will follow you blindly? And how much do you know about handling people? There are matters political in general. No! You are raw, free, uncouth and, right now useless to Mercia, whether you like it or not!'

Wulfhere flinched and broke eye contact. His heart shrivelled, and he scowled to hide his feelings, yet a part of him was honest. He recognised truth when it was thrown at him. He had a flashing vision of his father, overseeing tribal matters, and it dawned upon him how wise he had been, how knowledgeable about their customs and law.

'I'll not go alone. I want Osburga with me as my wife!' he stated flatly.

'You can't have her, you young fool. She's within the prohibited degrees for marriage. You are sixth cousins and a match would be banned automatically. Anyhow, in the morning she'll have gone to be betrothed elsewhere, with a magnificent dower that you could never match and a Morning Gift of similar quantity. So you can forget her for starters!'

Horror filled Wulfhere's eyes, and his shoulders slumped. In all his wild passion and enthusiasm he had completely forgotten his distant relationship with Osburga's family. He felt as if blows rained on his back from all directions. He leaped to his feet and stamped about the little clearing with frustration.

Burhred watched with amusement. Oh youth, he thought! Everything is so black and white. Had he been the same? It was all so long ago, he found it difficult to remember. Then his heart hardened.

'Sit down and grow up a bit!' he cried angrily. 'I have something better than to sit here all day and watch your juvenile tantrums. You think you are fit to be king when you act like this? Spare me!'

Wulfhere turned to snap a curse at the elder, then commonsense stopped him as well as the open mockery in Burhred's eyes. He walked back and squatted down on his heels once more.

'All right! I'm listening!' he said in a more humble voice.

Burhred was mildly surprised. The boy had acted much better than he had thought possible, so he carefully related all that which he and his two allies had planned. Wulfhere heard him out thoughtfully. He had to admit it all made sense, and he chewed the solution reflectively until a point occurred to him.

'Forgive me,' he said softly. 'You are a very old man. What happens if you should die before—?' and he left the question hanging.

Burhred was delighted. This was a good example of straight thinking, and he felt a new flash of warmth for this rebellious prince. 'Apart from the other elders, my companions, my servant Oswald knows everything and as you may have suspected he is a first-class man totally loyal to me only. The companion I've picked to be your tutor is called Aidan, and I've known him many years. He's thirty, without any family ties and is all for Mercia and me. You will be hidden in a tiny little place where no one will possibly think of looking for you, because no one knows it exists!'

Suddenly Wulfhere felt a flash of enthusiasm at the thought he was going somewhere new and strange. Anything would be better than staying here with his elder brother ruling.

'What if something happens and we want to get in touch with you urgently?' he wanted to know.

Burhred was delighted. 'Good thinking!' he praised. Long ago he had learned how to w ield the carrot and stick in appropriate proportions. 'I shall arrange for an extremely trustworthy courier to ride down to you now and again. I will see that your companion has a code for writing, which can be used safely. Do you remember that old cave I showed you long ago?'

Wulfhere nodded. 'I sometimes go there when I want to be alone to think,' he confessed. 'I don't think anyone else knows about it.'

Burhred agreed it was a ride of at least five miles in a direction that had little attraction for anyone because the hunting was not good.

'Go and take yourself there and wait until the churl arrives. Do not leave the area. If by bad luck anyone should wander in that direction, hide yourself. You have disappeared. Aidan, when he comes, will arrange for your suitably blood-covered tunic to go to a place where it can be found. Everyone will agree you are dead, which will take the pressure off me for a long time. It's spring, so we'll have you killed by a boar. There is a sounder not far away, and the sow has young, so they can take the blame!'

Wulfhere had nothing to say. Too much was happening too quickly. He was very uneasy about this stranger who was going to take over his life. What if he did not like him? Yet he dared not air this worry. He knew perfectly well Lord Burhred would resort to biting sarcasm, and, quite suddenly, it was important Burhred thought well of him. He wriggled his shoulders and managed a wry grin. 'I never thought it was going to be so hard to become a king!'

Burhred relaxed. He stood slowly, flexed his knees and collected his horse and mounted very slowly. 'Your churl Aidan will wear this ring as identification. Examine it!' he ordered.

'How will he know me?'

Burhred gave a wolfish grin. 'He will, and then he'll make mincemeat out of you initially!' he promised.

Wulfhere looked a little helplessly up at the

elder who understood. Being alone voluntarily was one thing, but having it enforced was another. He looked hard into the young man's eyes, wanting to say something wise and helpful but, for once, all the clever words vanished. 'Stay hidden and obey me, if you really do wish to be King of Mercia like your late father.'

The elder turned his horse, and without a backwards glance rode off. He could only hope that his harsh and caustic sentences had been understood. He pushed his horse into a canter. He was tired through to his bones and his joints ached. He wanted to get home to Oswald and wished he could lead a more peaceful life but this was the price he had to pay for his superior rank.

He gave a knowing nod to Eanwulf and Ealstan, as he dismounted in the tun. 'Don't know where he's got to this time.'

His allies were quick to pick up his ploy. 'Fishing somewhere?' Eanwulf asked, with just the correct amount of disinterested drawl in his voice.

Ealstan was not to be outdone. 'Most likely mooning over some girl,' he added.

Burhred grunted at them. 'And I wash my hands of that boy!' he stated irritably. 'I have something better to do with my time than run after Wulfhere!' he said in a voice loud enough for nearby people to hear.

There was a small knot of men congregated

by them. 'I agree with you, my lord. He is nothing but a born troublemaker. His disappearance is hardly a loss to any of us!'

Then another voice chipped in. 'He is royal though!'

'But with bad blood. Good riddance to him!' another said equally loudly.

Burhred handed his horses reins to a slave, threw a meaningful look to the two allies and they followed him into his home. It was a good house and comfortable. There were tanned animal skins on the floor, which would shortly be lifted, and hung up to air and dry. New dried rushes would be laid, which would smell sweet and inviting. He had a small hall, which opened into a larger room with sleeping cubicles on the left for three people. The fire always burned at the extreme end for cooking as well as warmth. Around the back were the tiny sleeping quarters for the few slaves he kept.

He eyed it all with satisfaction. He had had two wives, both of whom had died years ago. The first had been barren. The second had given him two daughters neither of whom had lived beyond their fourth year. After that he had not bothered. He knew he was not highly sexed and could barely manage an erection at all now except on rare occasions when he simply called in a female slave.

Oswald eyed him thoughtfully. Now what kind of a mood would he be in? He was a few years younger than Burhred and was neither slave nor a servant. He was a companion to the older man, a sounding board for ideas, and between them was a good friendship, though neither would have admitted this. They were comfortable with each other, understood the other's foibles and accepted them with considerable tolerance. They were quite happy to spend an evening together, not talking a lot, just relaxed in each other's company.

Oswald was not an extra tall man, but he was brawny with huge shoulders and a deep barrel chest. He had made a fine figure when younger, and married, but his wife too was dead. He was distantly related to Lord Burhred, and both of them had drifted together in one of those casual relationships that bond for years. There were no secrets between them, because there was implicit trust.

'Get rid of everyone, especially the slaves. I want a long talk with you this evening!' Burhred told him in a low voice.

Oswald eyed him. 'Just a quick word. How did it go?'

Burhred smile. 'Far better than I ever dared to hope.'

'Just as well,' Oswald told him. 'While you were away some of Oswiu's men have come. They went into a huddle with Peada!'

'So, it's started and I suppose Peada was dancing attendance on them?'

'Something like that!' Oswald replied and pulled a face.

'Time! Time! We must have time!' Burhred grated.

'We do. Now come and eat and stop fussing. Time is on *our* side now!'

CHAPTER FOUR

Elfrida cried. She had struggled to control herself to no avail. Cynewulf stood alongside her and felt his own eyes watering as Sihtric's funeral pyre started to die down at last. As the chief mourners they had their father's helmet, war shield and spare weapons on the fire. His rings and other jewellery had been divided between the siblings by the elders. It was very important that the gods understood his rank when Sihtric joined the spirits. Was he with King Penda at this moment? It was a question in Elfrida's mind that bothered her. Would the dead King Penda understand the incredible ride her wounded father had made for Mercia? Then she reassured herself. There were no secrets from the spirits, so perhaps even now he had been rewarded.

Yet her heart ached. With his death, she felt alone and vulnerable. It was so different for her brother. He had his masculine friends. He had Alicia chasing after him, making an exhibition of herself in the process while she felt so alone and lonely.

She had no close friend. Before this it had never bothered her. She was too happy living with her honed skills in the wild lands, communing with the animals, which she much preferred, if the truth be told, to people who stuck knives between shoulders. If only her mother had lived—and, always at this point, her heart would swell with pain. She had only a vague memory of her lovely mother. During those vital, formative years, it was her father who had been both friend and parent. Now she had no one. All she did have was an admiration and tender feelings for Wulfhere but where was he?

It had swept through the tun he had vanished again, and Lord Burhred was furious with him. Not that anyone seemed to care. And where also was Osburga? That was another mystery, which piqued her. One day she had been present, the next she had ridden off escorted by some men with a rumour flying around she was betrothed to another in a neighbouring town twenty miles away. Did Wulfhere's disappearance have anything to do with this? Surely his sudden vanishing act could not be serious or connected with his father's death? If only there was someone she could ask.

Lord Burhred would know, because he knew everything she reminded herself. The trouble was he could be so crusty and bad-tempered. She hesitated to go to his home, then she saw Oswald and brightened. He was preparing to ride off somewhere. The pyre was nearly out, and the ashes would be taken away and buried. She knew she did not want to see this. Let Cynewulf supervise something for once.

Elfrida turned and broke into a fast walk. She liked Oswald very much. He was the nearest to an uncle she had, and she would dearly love him at this moment as friend and confidant, yet she thought she was going to be too late. Oswald mounted, spun his horse around on its hocks, then trotted briskly away. Now where was he going and why?

She eyed Burhred's home, thought a moment, then walked over to it. She studied the open door and, peeping in, managed to see him sitting taking a drink and eating. She coughed extra loud, waited and repeated this.

Burhred did not hear the first cough because he was so engrossed in complicated thoughts compounded by enormous worries. What if something went wrong? He was too wise to make the error of thinking every plan was foolproof. And no matter how he examined his problem from every angle, he could not be wholly certain he had allowed for every eventuality. There was always the hidden, the unsuspected which could rear its head when least expected. He had no doubts at all about Aidan. He did not think he needed to worry too much about Wulfhere once Aidan was with him. What did needle him was the way Peada had started to flaunt himself before the Northumbrians and sway his people. Mercians, acquiescent! For how long though, he pondered? He knew his tribe. They would stand so much and not one step more, but just how long would it take for Peada's odious behaviour to sicken the proud Mercians?

He did hear the second artificial cough and swung around to stare through his propped open door. The day had been gorgeous, with the sun shining in, and some of the usual winter wetness was disappearing from floors and walls. He was surprised at this interruption. People usually made an appointment to see him, except for his two close companions. They were free to come and go as they liked, accepted by all the people as being three old friends of many years standing.

He was taken aback to see it was Sihtric's daughter. 'What do you want?' he grumbled ungraciously.

Elfrida dithered uncertainly. Was that an invitation to enter? She plucked up her courage and stepped forward, halting before the elder. They eyed each other. The future and the past. Now she was here, Elfrida's words dried up, and she was conscious of Lord Burhred's hard stare. What cold eyes he had at times. They didn't so much look at a person as bore into their very heart. She felt a shiver slide down her spine and regretted this impulsive action.

Burhred was equally astonished. She had guts, he had to hand it to her. Who else among the young fry would dare to venture into his home like this? He took time to examine her more closely now. She was not bad-looking, he conceded, and she held herself with dignity and grace. Her eyes did not flinch from his, yet he could sense how her nerves were screwed up tight. He knew she was as bright as her stupid brother was solid. He reflected that he had never really taken the time to plumb her depths. Why should he? She was simply another young nonentity, or was she? He fancied something trickled across the periphery of his mind.

'Well?' he rasped and waited.

Elfrida took a deep breath. 'I've heard Wulfhere has vanished!' she started and wondered how to proceed next.

'So?'

She licked her lips. Attack from the flanks, she told herself. 'And Osburga has also gone and everyone knows Wulfhere fancied her!' There, she had managed to get that bit out.

Burhred sniffed. There was nothing private in this place. Why did this girl look as if she were on the verge of exploding with some pent-up emotion? Suddenly, he realised he had started to enjoy this unexpected confrontation. How sharp was she when put to the test? He had a flashback to himself when at her age, all false confidence tangled with raw insecurity. He softened his gaze, and let something twitch at his mouth corner.

'Osburga has gone to be betrothed to another, because Wulfhere was barking up the wrong family tree, wasn't he?'

Elfrida woke up. Of course, why hadn't she thought of that? 'But where is he?' she persisted. Burhred knew everything. Didn't he?

The elder's eyes narrowed. This girl seemed to display a one-track mind. 'What is it to you, girl?' he asked softly.

Elfrida took a deep breath and had no idea how to answer. She looked down at one boot, and idly scuffed it on the floor. 'Just wondered!' she floundered and wished she had not come now.

You little liar, Burhred told himself. You are more interested in our young hothead than is good for you and he swiftly reviewed her pedigree. It was sound, there was no disputing that but she still seemed very young emotionally. He suspected the girl was a natural loner, which, with her obtuse brother, was not surprising. Now with her father also gone she was virtually alone. She was a decent girl and had given no trouble, except that she too had a penchant for disappearing as and when she felt like it.

He decided to change tactics. 'Where do you go when you wander off alone, and why?' he asked, very gently now.

Elfrida lifted her head again. Why, Lord Burhred had altered once more. His eyes were soft and warm with genuine interest. She waved one hand around in a vague circle. 'I like to watch the animals, and I don't mind being alone,' she added wistfully. 'I like to study the plants and try to remember which can be used for healing and diet. I like to try and track the animals. That can be great fun, especially when they don't know I'm on their back trail,' she confided, and gave a little impish grin.

Burhred took all this in. Here was a spirit crying out for companionship, but only of the right kind. Wulfhere? How very interesting, but he guessed, one-sided. Perhaps Wulfhere had not even realised someone fancied him.

'You should mix more with girls of your own age.'

Elfrida snorted. 'Most are married and have a baby too!' she riposted carefully.

Now, it was the elder's turn to let out a snort of disapproval. 'That's all right, for someone who can do no better, but there are others, you are one, who are too good to marry young. Also, you have to be with the correct rank and status. The Witan would never agree otherwise!'

Wulfhere isn't just anyone, she screamed

51

silently. If only she knew where he was. Then she could ask this elder to think of speaking for her? She took a deep breath and knew she could confide nothing more. Obviously, he knew where Wulfhere was and he had no intention of saying. She puzzled about this for a few seconds and realised she should go. She gave a polite little duck of her head to him, threw him a wan smile and backed away.

After she had gone, Burhred started to think more carefully. Oswald was an excellent man totally reliable in all ways and he had a good head on his shoulders. Were there situations where a female might be more provident? It was a new thought upon which considerable reflection must rest. In the meantime let the girl wander and roam alone. No harm would come to her and once the news of Wulfhere's death broke, she would be back.

It took just seven days for this to happen and Elfrida did not stand upon ceremony this time. She almost burst into his home, startling Oswald, who was sharpening a spear.

'Manners, girl. You call out first!' he rebuked sternly.

Oswald caught Burhred's eyes, and tactfully took himself, the spear and a sharpening stone outside.

'I've heard he is dead!' Elfrida blurted out. 'I don't believe it!'

Burhred took his time to reply while he

weighed her up. She was obviously in a distraught state, with tears not far away. Her eyes were wild, and her well-formed breasts heaved as she took deep gasps of air.

'Control yourself, girl,' he said harshly. 'I will not have you charging in here in such a manner!'

Elfrida sank down on a stool uninvited, appalled at what she had done. 'I am sorry, but when I heard he was dead, so soon after my father—' and she shook her head with disbelief.

Burhred decided he had better make up the rules as he went along. 'Hunters do get killed and what animal is more savage, at this time of the year, when a boar and sow have young. You know perfectly well the sounder has been in this region for a while.'

Elfrida quivered. Her whole world had collapsed, and it was a struggle not to sit here and howl her misery. Without Wulfhere, lovely, wonderful Wulfhere what was the point of it all? 'But he'd killed boars before, for the meat!'

Burhred pulled a face. 'So have other hunters. They make one slip and it is their turn. His tunic is outside, ripped to shreds and covered with blood, so there is no mistake, because no one else is missing,' he lied smoothly from long, expert practice.

Elfrida felt tears slide down her cheeks, and she could not help it. He was gone, and there had not been one tender word between them, because he had never spoken to her. It was so cruel and unjust. She sniffed and bit her lip.

'There are other young men,' Burhred said kindly.

'Not like him!' Elfrida wailed. 'I loved him so much!'

Burhred nodded at this confirmation of his suspicions. 'What did he have to say about that?'

Elfrida peered through her tears. 'He didn't know I existed. It was all Osburga this and Osburga that, until I could have screamed!' she admitted heavily.

Burhred considered. That would be Wulfhere all over, because there were so many times when he failed to see what was under his nose when his one-track mind was elsewhere. Was this providential, though? He eyed the girl. She would get over it; she had to. A list of eligible male names slid through his mind as potential suitors, but he dismissed them one after the other. This girl needed a special young man.

Elfrida stopped crying, and rubbed her eyes. It had been the shock as much as the distress at her loss. She looked wanfully at the elder and saw how steady was his gaze. Then something entered her head. She tilted it to one side and frowned dubiously. It was true that such a very old man must have seen death many times, and even become used to it, yet it was peculiar that he was not upset. Was it because he was a skilled actor?

Burhred wondered what was going through her mind now but he applauded her control. She sat more correctly. The tears had dried, yet why did she stare at him so intently? He felt vaguely uncomfortable.

'What is it, my dear girl? Have I grown two heads all of a sudden?'

Elfrida did not reply. She frowned, her eyes narrowed, while her mind switched into rapid thought. Various permutations slid through her head as she weighed up pros and cons, tallied them with what she knew of their tribe's current situation, and reached a total, which astounded her.

'He is not dead, and you know this,' she blurted out in a little rush of words.

Burhred went cold, and his face changed to a hard mask, as his eyes narrowed, with the pupils turning into dots of ice. '*What* do you mean by that?' he barked coldly. Surely she was not that clever or had she just made a lucky guess? 'Answer me!'

Elfrida took a long, slow breath and nodded to herself. 'I think I see it all!' she murmured more to herself than him. 'For some reason, which I do not yet understand, you want people to think he's dead, but he still very much alive!'

Burhred cursed soundly to himself. How many others could have worked this out? He stood and slammed his door shut and flashed a look around. Oswald would have chased out the house slaves to ensure their privacy, which was a plus point but how to handle this girl?

'You don't answer, which means I'm right!' Elfrida whispered. Burhred's action with the door had not escaped her. 'And it's important that no one else knows. For some very good reason you certainly do not want Peada or the Witan, let alone the ordinary people, to know anything about this, because—?'

She paused: Peada was his brother. Yet she knew there had been little love between them, barely tolerance. 'I have it! You think if Wulfhere had stayed here, someone might have harmed him. He is too young just yet to be our king so you have sent him somewhere safe where he can grow and learn!'

Burhred was thunderstruck and furious. He felt frustrated rage rise in his throat and was lost for words for once. He could only glower back at her and Elfrida simply beamed at him. Her smile widened and her eyes filled with joy, so vivid that Burhred felt his rage evaporate. He saw the danger and reverted to his angry self.

'His life is now in your hands, girl,' he said with ice in his tone. 'You let just one word slip, and you are as good as signing his assassination. Only four other people, apart from us, know. Really I should kill you here and now,' and it was no idle threat.

Elfrida sensed this, but was unafraid. 'I give you my oath, as the daughter of Sihtric, no one will ever learn anything from me for the simple reason I adore him!'

'I don't like it,' Burhred muttered. 'A secret should be known only to one person. Five makes a very high number. That brother of yours, with his loose tongue and thick head, must be the last person to know anything!' he warned coldly.

Elfrida nodded. 'I agree with you, my lord. Cynewulf certainly isn't bright enough to work out something like this!'

From being broken-hearted, she felt renewed with hope and she had confidence in her own ability to stay utterly silent at all times.

Burhred weighed her up and knew he had to believe her. They eyed each other, uniting with the secret of another person's life. They both wanted the same object for different reasons, but were on the same path.

'Now get out of here and get off my back, girl, unless you want a thundering hiding. Don't come here again unless I send for you!' he snarled as Elfrida decided it would be politic to vanish immediately.

Burhred let out a stream of curses, as Oswald came back in. He related the conversation, which his friend considered.

'Give her a chance,' Oswald advised sagely. 'She might just yet be useful. She would make a good courier being female, because she is well-known for vanishing as and when she fancies. No one would miss her!'

Burhred swore again. 'Confounded girl has given me a shock!' he grumbled.

Oswald knew him of old. 'You'll get over it!' Actually, the old boy was thriving on it all.

* * *

Wulfhere did not thrive on his shock. He had obeyed the elder's orders to the letter, then found the time dragged with boredom. Initially there had been a lot to do. He had to reach the cave unseen, make himself comfortable, and ensure he had enough meat, which meant hunting. He had his bow but this was really only suitable for small game. It would be many centuries before the advent of the lethal longbow. His spear, with its very long shaft, was the superior weapon, and at close quarters he had a dangerously sharp dagger and a small sword.

Once he had seen to his creature comforts he fell a prey to gloomy thoughts, which tangled up together. It was the very first time in his life he had been compelled to live alone night as well as day. It never entered his head that this was another deliberate tactic of Burhred—a period of grave reflection, with no one in whom he could confide. It was a make or break week in which he had to come to terms with the present and future. This had to be done alone and, cunning Burhred calculated that by the time Aidan arrived, Wulfhere would be delighted for company, any company, even that of a harsh disciplinarian.

Wulfhere was furious over Osburga, and he realised he had made a crass fool of himself in the elder's eyes. He writhed when he remembered the elder's words, and how Osburga must have led him on for her own amusement. Girls, he thought moodily! They are not worth bothering with. Certainly not when he had so much at the personal stake of ambition and rank.

He even felt humiliated. How dare Lord Burhred consider him little more than a child, where weapons and fighting was concerned. It was true, he admitted honestly, he had never fought in battle but how could that be held against him? What exactly was so wonderful about this teacher, and how dare anyone think he required tuition? His thoughts rumbled from the belligerent to the dismal, but he was young and healthy. He slept soundly at night, tucked into his thick cloak. He tried to keep himself bodily clean with a fastidiousness common to the Saxons, although this fell far short of the Roman standards centuries ago.

On the seventh day at noon his sharp ears picked up an unusual sound, and instantly he was on his feet, nerves alert. The sound came from the north so he bolted towards a cover of

59

some thick trees. Whoever was coming was a terrible woodsman. Their progress was both louder and careless and Wulfhere smiled to himself. It was either the elder or this famous churl of his and, if the latter, he was a heavy, flat-footed bear who could startle no one.

The steps plodded nearer, and twice he heard the sound of metal hitting wood, which puzzled him. He grinned maliciously, slipped an arrow against his bow string and waited when the riderless horse appeared, plodding forward a little aimlessly.

At the same second, he heard the shrill, very high-pitched whistle, which meant instant death. He reacted instinctively and flung himself sideways, rolled into frenzied action and his swift reflexes propelled him to his feet as he leapt behind another bush.

The arrow thudded into the tree against which he had stood, its feathers quivering. Wulfhere gasped as his heart hammered against his ribs; and then another whistle but from where? The second arrow knifed into the moist earth at his feet. He was galvanised again, leapt a bush and rolled himself down flat in thick, moist grass. He had dropped his bow in a shock, but dare not go for it.

He lay frozen with fear. The horse lowered his head and noisily started to crop at the grass. A bird flew overhead, with an annoyed chatter, then a third whistle. This one landed with a neat plop two feet from his left wrist.

He knew he must move again. The enemy had his position and range. He jumped to his feet, spun on his toes, vaulted a low shrub and shot down a track, intending to put distance between himself and this enemy until he could work out a plot.

He bounced off a tree trunk, half turned when huge arms pinioned him and he was lifted aloft like an infant and tossed into the air. He landed heavily, all the wind driven from his lungs. The man looked down at him jeeringly, then mocked with a grating laugh.

Wulfhere's volatile temper exploded. He snatched his dagger, holding it low for the upwards gutting stab and flung himself forward. The man waited calmly, and, almost casually, blocked the knife thrust and kicked out hard. His booted foot landed on Wulfhere's balls. He screamed and collapsed, bent double, writhing in an agony he had never dreamed existed.

Very slowly, he staggered erect, still bent forward, clutching his scrotum. The man was merciless. He grabbed Wulfhere's hair, hauled his head back and with one free hand slapped him hard, first on one cheek then on the other. 'You are nothing but a useless infant,' he snapped, 'and I'm expected to make a king of such material? What a pathetic joke,' he sneered.

Then Aidan flung Wulfhere from him as if he were tainted and stood with his hands on his hips, eyeing him carefully. He had not wanted this job. He did not want any job come to that. He was free, well off, with adult children, who had started to give him grandchildren and life was rosy. It was also very boring.

When Oswald had explained in detail, Aidan's inclination was to refuse out right but he remembered: long ago, he had owed his life to Burhred, a debt still outstanding. 'Why me?'

Oswald knew him of old and admired his independent spirit. 'Because I cannot think of anyone else with the right qualities who has a still tongue!'

Aidan had no answer to that, and both of them knew it. 'Is this kid worth bothering with though?'

Oswald drank the ale, which Aidan had hospitably offered when taking him into his home. 'Can you see Burhred wasting his time on a nonentity?'

'No!' Aidan had been forced to admit and knew all about Peada. 'Give me all the details and how much time I will have!'

Oswald told him everything, which Aidan considered very carefully. It might prove interesting, though he had never considered himself as a king maker. On the other hand, he knew if he stayed here much longer, he would stagnate. He would then only go out and pick a fight with someone for the sheer hell of it. His fine, healthy sons and their families managed quite nicely without him, so he nodded. 'You are on, but I use my methods, and they'll not be dainty ones either!'

Oswald had chuckled. 'All the better! This boy has potential, but he wants a thrashing or two!'

Now Aidan casually flashed the unusual ring on his finger and Wulfhere started. 'Aidan?'

'The same—and now, boy, when I tell you to jump, you jump or have I been landed with a namby-pamby?'

Wulfhere pulled himself up straight. The pain in his scrotum had eased and for the very first time in his life he felt genuine fear of another human being. He was so enormous, and it was not just height alone. He was big. His shoulders were great, he had a barrel chest, and his bare arms, showing from a sleeveless tunic, bulged with the largest muscles he had ever seen. What was also staggering was the swift way such a large man moved on his feet and always balanced too!

An aura came from him, which attracted and repelled. One was good while the other threatened harm. The face was handsome in a rugged way, and he put the man's age somewhere between thirty and forty. The eyes of grey were filled now with mocking amusement and the proud head was held stiffly erect, supported by a thick neck with bulging muscles and tendons.

'Try me!' Wulfhere managed to get out, controlling his breathing slowly.

Aidan chuckled. 'I intend to.' He paused. 'And if I find you wanting in any way you're finished!' he stated coldly. 'We understand each other?'

Wulfhere gulped and nodded. 'Yes, Aidan!' he replied, then his natural honesty showed. 'I wasn't expecting all that!' he admitted.

Aidan was pleased but did not show it. At least the boy had not whimpered or whined, which was something on which to work. 'A king has to be prepared for anything and everything at any time of the day or night,' he explained slowly. 'And he always protects his balls!'

Wulfhere grimaced. 'I'll not forget that!'

Aidan relaxed a little. 'Let's get back to your cave, and I'll explain in detail what Lord Burhred has planned, and the first thing is to have that tunic ripped and covered in blood so everyone considers you dead. In my saddlebags are churl's clothes for you, because from now on that is your rank. You'll go by the name of Hoel. It's a good common one. And you have become my kid brother, travelling with me, recovering from a bad illness. Wulfhere no longer exists until Lord Burhred decides otherwise and that might take considerable time. At least two years!'

Wulfhere nodded understandingly, still very much in awe of this man, but also a little chagrined at his treatment. For the first time, he was aware his confidence had taken a brutal hammering and he eyed the churl doubtfully. Was more of the same in store? He took a deep breath and managed to straighten without wincing. If this was what it took to be a king, so be it, he would go through with it because he realised there was no other alternative.

Before they left the next morning, Aidan eyed his pupil. 'Strip!' he barked and studied Wulfhere's body as he stood, skin goose-pimpled at dawn. He went around the young man, deciding which muscles need to be developed first. The potential was there but work and time were certainly needed.

'Right!' he grunted, as they mounted up. 'Once we are away from this immediate area I shall trot or slow canter and you will run alongside. I've never seen such skinny legs in all my life! A warrior, especially a king, must have strong, well-muscled legs, which he can stand on to face the world. Yours will do on a maiden!'

Wulfhere pulled a face, but kept his lip shut tight. He had a nasty, sneaky feeling he was going to be worked worse than a slave but he had a bit of a sense of humour, and threw a wry grin at his trainer.

In a way, he was sorry to say goodbye to the cave. It had been a sanctuary, and he vowed to himself that the day he became king, he would come back to reflect and remember.

He wore drab common trousers and tunic, without any ornamentation. From his waist belt hung a utilitarian knife, and in his right hand, a plain spear. His shield was fastened to the back of the saddle with a quick release knot. It was a round, wooden orb with a strong centre boss. The whole had been covered with black leather, and behind the boss was a hollow, which allowed the knuckles to grip firmly at the inside strap.

Aidan was similarly clad, but had a short javelin and an equally short throwing axe. At the rear of his saddle was a great battleaxe, a vicious heavy weapon obviously a copy of one from the Vikings. As he studied this latter weapon he appreciated the enormous arm muscles that would be required to wield such a weapon in battle for any length of time.

He had his bow and arrows in a quiver. As the son of a king he was entitled to a long, ornate sword, a weapon of a noble. As a churl, which he now was, this was not allowed.

'Why don't you carry a sword?' he asked curiously, as they rode abreast.

Aidan shrugged. 'I could, I was given permission a long time ago for battle exploits, but it is not my best weapon! Now dismount and start to run alongside. Regulate your breathing. Use your arms, and don't waste breath trying to talk to me!'

Wulfhere had considered himself fit and tough. He received a rude awakening, but jogged on obediently until he was covered in sweat, and his breath rasped heavily. His legs became limp, and when he began to wobble, his trainer let him mount up again.

Wulfhere wondered why such a splendid man as this had not been invited to join his father's Gesith, his personal bodyguard. But he had no breath left to start asking questions. Although it was a great honour to join a Gesith, a refusal was never held against a man. Perhaps Aidan was a bit of a loner?

When both were mounted, Wulfhere was quite glad to ride in silence. He felt utterly exhausted, already. Now and again Aidan pointed out places of interest.

'Over there was a big fort when the Romans were here and at one time Publius Ostorius Scapula was stationed there when Governor of Britain. A hard, tough man. Down below is a small vil and where we're going is just beyond it. Leave all the talking to me!' he ordered.

It would soon be night and they had ridden a long way at a punishing pace for his legs. For nearly half of it he had loped alongside his horse, led by Aidan.

They dropped downwards, crossed a small river and came to a collection of miserable huts, suitable only for cattle or slaves. Only one dwelling stood proudly aside with a cattle pound on the left and a fenced area for horses to the right. It was an untidy, almost ugly little place, and they stayed on their mounts and waited.

Shortly a man came out to them, armed with a spear, some slaves behind him holding hounds. 'I am the lord of this manor!' he announced pompously.

'Aidan of Glevum travelling with my younger brother, Hoel, who has been ill and will be staying here with me to recover.'

The lord's eyes swivelled from one face to the other and they both received a sullen nod. 'You are welcome!' they were told and both of them sensed a blatant lie.

Wulfhere felt himself prickle but sat still and mute. So this was a Hwicce! A vassal of Mercia! He felt something twinge in his guts; this was now how his people were to King Oswiu.

'You are expected,' the lord continued solemnly and Wulfhere wondered if this was his usual mien, then he silently applauded Lord Burhred's crafty planning.

Aidan threw him a hard look. 'Who lives at Gete?' he demanded hectoringly.

'A handful of slaves,' the lord replied, unable to hold eye contact, but finally he looked up. 'You staying long?' he asked hopefully.

'As long as it suits!' Aidan shot back, laying the ground rules at once. 'You are Cyneard?'

The other nodded and broke eye contact again, though his whole body language screamed resentment and bottled anger.

Wulfhere needed no tutor on this and he watched the sullen man warily before shooting a look at Aidan. The older man sat like a rock, cold-faced, harsh-voiced as he enforced his personality on the lord.

'I believe Ethelhelm is your undertaking?' Aidan asked with icy meaning.

Wulfhere understood. This would be the man's son now held as hostage for their lives. No wonder he was so sullen, almost trembling with barely contained fury.

Cyneard nodded again, and he dared to meet Aidan's eyes. 'He is only ten years!'

Aidan gave him back a very straight answer. 'Let us hope he lives to see eleven years then!'

Cyneard flinched, lowered his gaze, beaten like a cur. It entered Wulfhere's mind to wonder exactly where Oswald had taken the boy but he dismissed the question as irrelevant to his situation.

Aidan continued to tighten the screw. 'You and your family are well, I trust?' he asked, grimly.

Cyneard's anger flared showing in sudden red cheeks, but he dared do nothing. He forced himself to be restrained. One look at this battle-hardened churl had warned him where he stood, which was on very thin ice indeed. This churl would kill as quickly as breathe. He wondered about the younger brother. From where had they come exactly, why or what did they intend to do on his manor? But he kept his mouth wisely shut. The odds were too heavily stacked against him. At present.

'My hospitality is yours,' he managed to get out reluctantly.

Aidan shook his head. 'We'll camp a mile away and we'll need someone to cook!'

Cyneard blinked and thought a moment, then nodded. 'Give me a minute, Lord!' he said, elevating Aidan's rank with a fawning gesture. He returned after a few moments, dragging a young slave girl with him. She carried her hastily gathered few possessions. 'She needs taming,' he said bluntly.

The girl hung her head and Wulfhere's nose twitched. She stank. Her clothing was filthy, her skin coated in dirt and her hair of an uncertain colour, because of filth and grease. She was small, thin, pathetic and terrified.

Cyneard continued pointing at the girl. 'I bought her and her father last year. She needs a firm hand, her name is Egwina. She might do as a bedmate for your brother. I tried her out myself, but she isn't to my taste.'

'We'll take her,' Aidan replied to Wulfhere's surprise. They could manage very well on their own so why have a third party let alone this filthy, stinking girl? He guessed Aidan had an ulterior motive, and he set his mind to work. He had a good one when he chose to use it in the correct manner, and he thought he understood. Tame the girl and she would talk about this miserable lord and give Aidan a clue as to his reliability, despite his son being held hostage.

'Walk ahead of us,' Aidan said, but not unkindly. 'Now that way.'

The two rode in silence, after a sharp warning look from Aidan; then he concentrated on walking around, eyeing the general terrain. It was only a small river, with good grassland on either side, and part of it was still quite heavily forested. The river's muddy banks showed that it was capable of overflowing after a lot of rain, with many grasses and reeds growing for quite a considerable distance. It was a nothing place, yet Wulfhere sensed it was a peaceful one. The thought of spending at least two years here was depressing. Then he made himself brighten up at the knowledge of the reward to come. There were two slave huts set at an angle and then the land rose a little.

'We'll make our camp on top of that slope. We'll build a rough lean-to for temporary accommodation, then slaves can build a proper house for the bad weather. Not a pit house, either, one with a wooden floor.'

As they unsaddled and hobbled their mounts Wulfhere eyed the girl. She stood with a sullen look on her face or was it barely controlled fury? For a few seconds, something rippled down his spine and he frowned, then strolled over to the churl. 'I don't like her!' he

71

said and patted his guts. 'She gives me a bad feeling here!'

Aidan was instantly alert. 'Is that so?' he drawled carefully. Instinct was something never to be ignored. 'You, girl, make yourself a bed under that tree!'

Egwina turned, every muscle shrieking objection, yet she said not a word. Aidan drew Wulfhere aside. 'I intend to pump her dry in due course, because trust that Lord I do not, with or without a hostage against him!'

Wulfhere nodded, pleased with his personal deductions. There were some movements from the slave huts they had passed and a man and a woman appeared, to stand watching hesitantly. Aidan waved a hand brusquely, and they hastened over to drop on their knees before him.

'Names!' Aidan barked imperiously.

The man looked at him white-faced with fear. 'I am Alcium, and this is my woman called Edith,' and his voice quaked.

Wulfhere guessed they could not be many years older than himself. In their mid-twenties. They were in as filthy a condition as the girl, and he frowned. It was common sense to look after slaves, because they cost money, they were property. This couple were too thin. Their cheek bones stood out in stark relief and their faces were gaunt.

'Do you look after the cattle?' Aidan asked and waved a hand to where some stock grazed.

Alcium replied quickly. Strangers terrified him, because they were the unknown quantity, which could mean danger and distress for the likes of him and Edith. He hastened to please. 'Yes, lord!'

He and Edith lived as a man and wife, away from the vile-tempered Cyneard, and now their peace was shattered. Who were these two and why were they here? But he dared not question. Slaves could only accept.

'Tomorrow you will leave those animals and build a proper house. For me and my brother. My orders over-rule any others you may have been given. We shall hunt tomorrow, and there will be meat for you,' he said, recognising starvation when he saw it. 'This girl will help. I look after slaves, if they look after me and mine!' and Aidan emphasised his last words.

Alcium brightened and caught his breath. Dare he hope this was the start of something better? He nodded, and his shoulders slumped with relief.

CHAPTER FIVE

Elfrida stood frozen, doubting her ears. 'You what?' she shouted angrily. 'How dare you!'

Cynewulf faced her, feet apart, smugly sure of himself. 'I am the only male, and that makes me the head of the family so you have to do as

I say!' he started arrogantly. Alicia was right. Why hadn't he listened to her before, and King Peada, like the good Christian he was, would most certainly approve.

'Get stuffed!' Elfrida spat back at him, quivering with anger. She stepped forward, drew back her right fist and let fly. Cynewulf was totally unprepared and her blow caught him flush on the point of his jaw. He went flying backwards to land heavily on his seat.

Alicia watched from a discreet distance and was appalled. Elfrida did just as she liked, but now that Wulfhere was dead she should be married and who better was there now than a Northumbrian? She had worked out that this would please their new king, give Cynewulf a splendid chance to inveigle himself into the king's good favour and draw attention to both of them. Perhaps their rank would be enhanced, because Alicia was a natural social climber. The fact she came from a respectable family of churls was neither here nor there. She wanted Cynewulf, but, more, she wanted him elevated to the nobility. She was disappointed he had not been invited to join the new king's gesith, but she would work something out in due course. Cynewulf, darling as he was, did need a push now and again. The first thing was to remove that odious Elfrida who seemed to come and go as she liked. She was far too familiar with Oswald and Lord Burhred. She was also disrespectful to her brother.

Elfrida watched Cynewulf lumber to his feet, sparks shooting from his eyes, his mouth opening, so she moved first. With a speed he did not know she possessed, she kicked out with her right boot. Then she hooked around his left ankle and Cynewulf went flying for a second time. With a snort of derision, Elfrida turned on her heel and stormed off.

She knew she must be alone, until her temper cooled down, and she broke into an easy trot. She was very fit and knew her area well but after a while, quite away from the tun, she spotted a small track and branched off. This was somewhere new, and she trotted uphill, wondering where she was going to come out. It was a long, upwards track, very narrow, and she noted rarely used, though someone had been here with a horse quite recently.

She padded the last few paces, feeling a little tired, because she guessed she had come quite a long way. She looked around with keen interest and came into a minute clearing, which held a cave and her eyes opened wide with amazement. She had had no idea there was one here, and she walked forward, eyes studying the ground carefully. It was obvious that someone had been here, and more than one. A quick effort had been made to obliterate signs of occupation, but they were screamingly obvious to her sharp, highly trained eyes. She stepped into the cave, and her eyebrows shot upwards.

It was a good cave. The ceiling was not too high, but it went back far enough for any occupant to be quite sheltered from the worst weather. She strolled around as a tiny suspicion started to grow. There had been a fire here, and though it had been kicked apart, she read, it was not all that old. She found a bone, took it out to the light and knew it was from a young deer. Outside she paced around. Aidan's work had been done in too much of a hurry to fool a skilled tracker like herself and she returned to the cave, entered, sat down and started to think seriously.

This was a delightful hideaway, and she resolved to have it as her own bolt-hole. When she did go back to the tun she would take care to obliterate her tracks very thoroughly, as well as hide the entrance to the path. With a good digging stick, she would swiftly replant some small shrubs, then only she would know of the place.

It was obvious this was where Wulfhere had been hidden, which meant Lord Burhred also knew! Now was a good time for reflection. Cynewulf's attitude no longer surprised her. Alicia was at the back of it all and, thinking deeply, she worked it all out.

There were now three Northumbrian men in their tun who had been closeted with the king for ages. When they emerged they had conducted a very serious census of every home. The head of each family had been forced to identify himself, and Elfrida had noticed very little was missed. Neither was it committed to memory. Copious writing had taken place, and it hadn't taken much brain work to understand why. These ghastly Northumbrians were figuring out the exact tribute her tun would have to pay to King Oswiu based upon the number of inhabitants, their goods, capital and everything else.

It was dreadful. Was it possible that King Peada had thought out a new idea where all single people were to be paired off and married, especially to Northumbrians? Girls usually went to boys' tuns, so, inevitably, half of her tun's population would be in Northumbria. In turn, Mercia would never be able to rise again. It was the old case of divide and rule. It was smart planning on someone's behalf. King Peada was no fool. He had married into Oswiu's family and adopted Christianity as the price.

By the time the Mercian people became fed up with this they would be too weak to revolt and take up arms, no matter how good Wulfhere might be when he returned. They would have been assimilated into Northumbria and vanished as a race.

She was a prime target with Alicia goading Cynewulf on. Although no girl could be forced to marry against her will, did this still prevail when a tribe were subjugated? She had no idea.

What could she do? Vanish? That would be difficult for a long period. How far did Northumbria's arms reach? She had overheard a snatch of conversation in which King Peada was going to be allowed by King Oswiu to rule all the land and people south of the River Trent, which was monstrous.

She knew she had to do something. Without parents or family, at her age, people would be bound to listen to Cynewulf.

A seed of an idea sprouted, and she considered it. It bore appeal and she smiled. Would he help? There was only one way to find out. Ask him! Quickly, she calculated her facts. She was fit, healthy, well-educated and sharp. She could also fight. She was an adept in the wild and would never need an escort, yet what could be the excuse? Think, she told herself.

Later that day, she returned to the tun. The path to the cave was firmly camouflaged, and she strolled, seemingly nonchalantly, towards Burhred's home. Again the door was open to let in brilliant sunshine but this time she called, remembering her manners and the elder's volatile temper.

Burhred was only half-surprised and not at all displeased to see her. He grinned at Oswald, who stood, stretched, then removed himself. Elfrida heard the slaves being sent outside, and when the elder beckoned, she stepped into his room and stood before him. Now that she was here her plan seem foolish in the extreme.

'Well?' Burhred asked. Now what was eating her? This girl was deep and complicated.

Elfrida sat as he indicated a stool, took a deep breath and shot it straight out. 'I want you to legally adopt me, sir!'

Burhred was thunderstruck, looked at her, and blinked. 'You what?' he managed to get out at last. This was one of those rare moments in his life when he was totally confounded. Then he snapped alert and grabbed his wits back into order. 'Why?'

Elfrida waited only a moment to collect her thoughts and assemble them in a coherent sequence. It would never do to be too emotional. 'To save me from a forced marriage to start with—a special horrible Northumbrian which my charming brother and that wretched Alicia appear to have been planning!' Then she explained her deductions in detail.

Burhred heard her out in silence and berated himself. Now his person had been drawn to these facts, he realised they were only too logical. He had been so heavily engrossed in his Wulfhere plan he had let his guard slip a little regarding the welfare of the tun in general.

'Yes, that would be a clever ploy, but King

Peada will have to get the whole of the Witan behind him for such a cracked-brain scheme. It's all King Oswiu's fault making Peada take up Christianity to marry into his family. We never had such problems here when we worshipped Woden, Thor or the other respectable gods. All this fuss and rubbish just because a man was crucified!' he grumbled, while he started to think carefully.

Elfrida forced herself to wait in silence. 'Please!' she breathed. 'I can turn to no one else!'

Finally Burhred shook his head and stared at her frankly. 'No! It wouldn't do and don't give me that poutish face. I've done you the courtesy of hearing you out, now you reciprocate!'

Elfrida bit her lip with disappointment, while her heart plummeted. It looked as if she would have to leave her tun and live an isolated, wild life. She shivered. Much as she did not object to her own company, being alone for an indefinite period, especially in the winter, was another matter entirely.

Burhred read her easily now and silently cursed the stupid Cynewulf and greedy Alicia. How was it possible that Mercia had bred such a fool as Peada?

'It's a good idea but it won't work,' he replied gently. 'Myself and my friends abstained on voting for Peada, and because of our defeat he did not have to fight for the position, more's the pity. You would be doing yourself a grave injustice to ally yourself with me. But there is one person who might adopt you and who would be acceptable!' he suggested coolly.

'Who?' Elfrida asked suspiciously.

'Oswald!'

'Oh!' and Elfrida blinked at this unexpected offer. She had always liked Oswald very much indeed, looking upon him as a kind of uncle. With him as adopted parent, she would be quite safe. 'He might not like the idea,' she pointed out sagely.

Burhred gave one of his famous sniffs. 'You let me talk to him. I can soon get the slaves to build an annex here for you and you would be with me, but not part of me. It would have to go before the king and the Witan, but as Oswald has no family of any kind, I cannot see any handicap.'

'That's fine with me but there is more. I don't want, even with adoption, to spend my days hanging around here so I thought—!'

Burhred stiffened and his voice went cold. 'If you think you have some harebrained scheme of riding to find Wulfhere, forget it! I won't have it! Is that clear?'

Elfrida, had the grace to blush. It was almost frightening how sharp this elder was. Could he read her mind?

'Wulfhere is safely ensconced a distance away, and there he stays until I decide

81

otherwise. If you turn up, or anyone for that matter from here, his cover is blown. It could even mean his death!'

Elfrida paled as this scheme dissolved into nothing. 'Oh!' was all she could manage.

Burhred felt for her. By all the gods did Wulfhere deserves such devotion? But he knew he must be very harsh. 'And what kind of girl are you to want to chase so flagrantly after a boy? Where is your pride and dignity!' he rebuked. 'And I thought better of you. Stop and think how Wulfhere would react if he learned that you intended to chase him!'

Elfrida looked down at her feet and cringed. She felt the protocol of tears hover near the back of her eyes and held her breath to control herself. Why was she so smitten with someone who did not even know she existed? She tried to defend herself. 'Alicia chases my brother!'

Burhred glowered at her. 'And makes herself look a fool in the process but then your brother is as bad.'

He watched her face, looked into her eyes and took a deep breath. Oh! The impetuosity of youth!

'When and if you do catch Wulfhere, you might not like what you snare!' he told her a little more kindly. 'There's also another point you have overlooked. Wulfhere left here as a boy. He will come back very much a man or a broken reed!'

Burhred decided she had taken more than

enough of his time. 'Later on, if you want to ride around, I might have some work for you. A task for Mercia that will require observant eyes, sharp ears, closed lips and a first-class memory.'

Elfrida perked up a little and gave him a brilliant smile. This sounded almost too good to be true but what could it be? She frowned and started thinking again.

Burhred let out an exasperated snort. 'Stop trying to read my mind!'

'You want someone trustworthy to ride around all our people and find out their views on paying tribute to Northumbria. And when they will be ready to take up arms against him!'

Burhred lifted one hand and shook his head. 'If you're like this now, then all the spirits help us when you are my age!'

'Am I right?'

'Of course you are!' he replied testily. 'But that won't be for another few months!' by which time, he told himself, she might have worked Wulfhere out of her system so he could have a bit of peace on such a volatile subject. If he was lucky, she might have met someone else. 'Now get out of here, and stop wasting any more of my time. If my friends are outside, send them in!' he ordered, meaning Eanwulf, Ealstan and Oswald.

Elfrida felt slightly pleased with herself and saw Ealstan. 'My lord Burhred wishes to speak to you and your friend,' she told him.

Ealstan nodded and turned direction. 'I don't know where Eanwulf is. I know he came back to change his clothing and was then going somewhere.'

Elfrida nodded, totally unconcerned, blissfully pleased with herself. She would go for a ride and have a little private celebration. This put her brother and Alicia well and truly in their place. She caught her favourite mount and trotted off, ignoring a few curious looks thrown in her direction. It would be good to get away and commune with her thoughts.

She cantered past a sentry at his post and took a path, almost a road, as it was the main one, which led to the forest fringe before it forked. She turned to the right, which led to higher land and a plain where trees gave way to short shrubs and flinty ground. It was a good place to ride and blow the cobwebs from face and mind.

Just before the last turning, she drew rein with surprise. There to one side stood a horse aimlessly cropping the grass as if starved, when she knew perfectly well their animals were as well fed as their slaves. She stopped and frowned, rather perplexed. When a horse behaved like that it could also indicate agitation.

Elfrida flung a look around. She had come out with only her dagger, which she knew was foolish. Something cold trickled down her spine as she peered over one particular shrub. Then she took a deep breath and dismounted. The body lay sprawled face down with a spear, prominent between the shoulder blades. Blood had poured in a stream, then coagulated as the man died.

The hair at the back of her neck tingled, and she flung a swift look around before approaching the body. Gingerly, she touched one arm. It still held warmth, so the man had not been murdered for long. She vaulted back onto her horse, whipped it around and galloped back the way she had come.

She left her horse loose and without ceremony, burst into Burhred's home. He, Oswald and Ealstan looked at her with astonishment.

Elfrida blurted out the words. 'My Lords, I have just found Eanwulf. He has been murdered!'

CHAPTER SIX

Wulfhere laboured as never before. He sweated in streams, as he forced himself to keep up with Aidan and was humiliated to find he could not. He had considered himself fit and strong, and he was embarrassed to discover otherwise. Aidan left him standing in every way, which made bitter medicine.

Aidan carefully watched the slaves erect a decent building with a wooden floor elevated from the earth by at least a handspan. The roof was to have a steep slope with upright timbers, ropes and rattans. Once the walls were up, they concentrated on making these watertight, and here Edith demonstrated her skill. It was she who filled the cracks with grasses and daubed the inside and out with thick mud. The fireplace went to one side with a slit to allow the smoke to escape. Tree bark made a circular cup to hold the wind from blowing smoke back down again.

Egwina worked with them, but she never spoke unless addressed first and then only in monosyllables. In between, Wulfhere and Aidan hunted each day and Egwina cooked, at which she was quite good. By dusk, everyone was exhausted. They had no inclination to linger or talk.

Twice Aidan had noticed a strange male ride into their area and view their labours before departing. They had just finished the house when Cyneard and his man came up. Aidan had been expecting this.

'Those two are my slaves!' Cyneard blustered. 'You've no right to use them without consulting me!'

Aidan looked him up and down, his gaze insulting, while Wulfhere stiffened into a posture of attack, should one come near. Egwina shrank away, terror on her face, which

Wulfhere did not miss. Alcium and Edith hung their heads, resigned to whatever might come next.

'Remember your position,' Aidan growled.

Cyneard flinched, coloured, made a fist of one hand, then reluctantly unfolded his fingers. Aidan dived into his tunic and pulled out a small drawstring purse, made from soft leather. He studied the contents, and then extracted certain coins. He strode over to Cyneard and slapped them into the startled man's hand.

'I've just bought them both, as well as this girl and some clothing for them. What they are wearing is riddled with lice.'

Cyneard glowered. 'They're not for sale.'

Aidan gave him a cold look. 'I didn't hear that. Now take my generous offering and leave *my* slaves to me and my brother and get off this land and stay off—if you wish to remain healthy!' he rasped.

'But I need them. My cattle—!' Cyneard bubbled with fury, but he had not missed Wulfhere's discreet move with a spear. With an oath he spun around and stormed away.

The three slaves huddled together and quivered with terror. 'Get on with the work. Brother, come with me!'

Wulfhere strolled with him until they were well out of earshot. 'He is trouble!'

Aidan nodded. 'I'm surprised when we hold his only son as hostage. There is more to this

87

than meets the eye. Did you see the look he flashed at Egwina too?'

Wulfhere started. 'Yes, but I think she was looking down at the time.'

Aidan faced him. 'There's something not quite right here!'

Wulfhere stood and pondered. 'It's a pity we can't get those slaves on our side,' he said, more to himself than his companion.

Aidan's eyebrows shot up approvingly. 'Now you are thinking like a king,' he said in a soft voice. 'What do you suggest?'

Wulfhere bit his lip. This was a big decision, and he felt the responsibility, yet he was pleased with Aidan's trust. He wished to give a worthy answer. 'If it was up to me, I'd free them.'

'Excellent!'

Wulfhere flushed with pleasure. 'If we free them they have an oath to give us, and the man could be our watchdog, his woman too but I'm uncertain about the girl. I sometimes think she has a very shifty look in her eyes.'

Aidan nodded encouragingly. 'You are using your head. That's good! So let's do it. Alcium, Edith! Here!'

Both of the slaves jumped, then ran over nervously. They halted before Aidan, and he regarded them carefully. 'You two stink. Your clothes are rotten. You are infested with lice. You are disgusting!'

Alcium went red, but he was not cowed. 'Sir,

it is not our fault. We've tried to keep clean, and the Lord did say we could have some skins but he changed his mind and said they were to be prepared as trade goods.'

'Are the skins in your huts? Good, get them and cut them up and make clothing and for this girl too. But before you put them on, get in the river and clean yourselves. You must know about herbs and soap root. From this moment on, you are free if you will give your oath to me and my brother.'

They froze with shock. Four eyes went from Aidan to Wulfhere and back again. To be free! They could hardly believe their ears.

Alcium never hesitated. He flashed a look at Edith, then took her hand and advanced. They bowed their heads to each man in turn. 'We give our oaths of loyalty to both of you, me and my wife!'

Wife, thought Wulfhere? It had been woman before. He exchanged a quick glance with Aidan, before they both smiled at the couple: 'You said—wife?' Wulfhere asked delicately.

Alcium hastened to explain. 'We are man and wife. We are—Mercians!'

'What?' Aidan and Wulfhere asked together. Mercians—as slaves? This was hideously appalling.

'What happened to you?' Wulfhere asked for both of them.

Alcium gave a heavy sigh. 'We had just

married when everything went wrong. My parents fell ill and died, and I was young and foolish. I spent what money I had offering prayers to the gods and buying medicine, and I ran hopelessly into debt. Gradually, I lost all I had and what was worse owed a lot of money. More than I could hope to recoup in years of labour. There was nothing I could do but sell myself into slavery to repay the debt,' he explained, holding Edith's hand. When he spoke again, his voice was choked. 'Edith could easily have divorced me and found another husband. Instead, she came into slavery with me, and we were lucky not to be separated.'

Aidan and Wulfhere marvelled at this devotion, something exceedingly rare. 'Did Cyneard rape you, Edith?' Aidan asked gently.

She managed a wan smile. 'He tried on the first night here. I just closed my legs and spat in his face. He thrashed me, so I spat again and again and again, and then I cursed him, calling upon all the gods. That frightened him very much. He tried another time with the same result but in the end gave it up and I was given all the filthy low jobs to do.' She paused to look to her husband. 'He took it out on my man as well, but we survived. We have had to!'

Aidan nodded his head to her. 'I salute your courage. Now will you serve me and my brother? There are many days when we shall be gone from dawn to dusk!'

'Gladly!' the two Mercians replied in unison.

Wulfhere marvelled at such love and loyalty. It flashed through his mind Osburga would not have stood by him in such a way. Osburga! This was the first time he had thought of her in a while. He examine his feelings honestly. There was no doubt Osburga would have lacked Edith's metal. If and when he ever did marry he wanted someone strong by his side like Edith.

Wulfhere walked a few paces with Aidan. 'If I ever marry, I want to experience that kind of relationship!'

Aidan smiled: 'In that case, you will have to be exceedingly lucky. Don't look for something you might never be destined to know. I speak from experience. I was happily married, but I can assure you, my wife was no Edith. She was a wildcat at times, though she could be fun as well. Just remember there is more to marriage than sex!' he said dryly.

They went riding, then, once they were out of sight of all possible watchers, Wulfhere dismounted and loped alongside his horse which Aidan led. They went for mile after mile, because now his young body had started to toughen up. When Aidan considered he had done enough of that he allowed him to mount and continue more exercises in the saddle.

'Warriors ride into battle, yet fight on foot, but the warrior whose body is really hard is the victor on the battlefield. We'll work like this for many weeks and then I want you to be perfection with every weapon known to man. At the same time, I shall examine your education. Always remember a king is not just a muscleman. He must understand his people and his tribe. He must be familiar with every custom. He must be able to handle his Witan, because he might not always agree with their advice. He will want to go his own way, so he must have a tongue persuasive enough to get everyone to agree with him! Even when they don't really want to!'

They finished the day's exercises by wrestling and Aidan went out of his way to use every dirty trick he knew. He wanted to try and make Wulfhere lose his temper. He nearly did succeed, but when they stopped to catch their breath Wulfhere glared at him. 'You fight dirty!'

Aidan laughed in his face. 'At least you kept your temper!' and this was almost an accolade.

Wulfhere grunted. 'I wondered if that was your game!'

'Good for you! Remember the man who openly loses his temper usually also loses the fight because he does not think straight. He leaves himself wide open, in one way or the other, and ends up rather dead!'

So they fell into a pattern, leaving the two free Mercians on watch. The slave girl did what work she was given, but remained mute, and almost sullen. Words could not be dragged from her so in the end the two Mercians left her alone. At least though, she cleaned herself up, wore fresh trousers and tunic and no longer crawled with lice. With the good, hunted meat, the three of them started to fill out, develop more energy and brighten up. It was just that the slave girl remained totally unreachable. Now and again she would go over to the manor house, to return with spices and herbs, and the Mercians noticed she would come back even more solemn and morose. They said nothing to their masters. It was not their way. Too long as slaves had taught them to be very careful what they said to anybody, especially those of a high rank.

When Aidan and Wulfhere returned one evening, after a violently strenuous day, they were astounded and put out to see a strange female working near their campfire. Both of their hackles arose but speech died away when they realised it was the slave girl.

She was totally transformed. During their absence, she must have been in the river and cleansed herself thoroughly, and now wore fresh clothing. Her hair was fair, and if it had not been for the constant sullen look she would have had a kind of beauty.

Wulfhere exchanged a look with his companion and grinned. It was the two Mercians who had set this example and they thoroughly approved. At least there were no more lice around or fleas to jump onto them.

Aidan signalled with his eyes and strolled a few paces away with Wulfhere. 'Well!' Aidan drawled. 'Is she clean enough for your bed now?' he asked with interest. 'Because if she is you can take her take her somewhere else. Not in our hut!'

Wulfhere paused, then gave Aidan a frank look. 'I'm not interested. I don't like that girl, dirty or clean. There is something about her that—' and he waved a hand dismissively, then grinned. 'By the time I've done a day's work with you, I'm too tired. Couldn't manage it at all!'

Aidan laughed. 'In that case, I still have work to do with you. I want you so hard and fit that you can fight all day and still perform half the night!' he leered. 'Tomorrow we will go for a long ride in another direction, and I'll examine what you know, mentally.'

Wulfhere pulled a face. 'Bit difficult to answer questions, while running alongside a horse!' he pointed out with amusement. He looked up at the churl, and his heart swelled with friendship and companionship. Already he looked upon Aidan as the brother he had not had and felt the camaraderie that can arise between two men, something totally different to anything between a man and a woman.

As usual they set off just after daybreak and rode at a steady trot for mile upon mile, going in a strange direction, due west. As they neared the mighty river, land began to change. It was marshy, with spongy soil and reeds proliferated.

The river was running full, backed by a high tide, and it had spilled over its banks for a considerable distance. Both men gazed at it with awe. It was enormously wide, and even from their distance they could see considerable turbulence caused by very fast moving currents.

'It's so huge!' Wulfhere murmured with amazement. 'I wouldn't like to fall in there. A man wouldn't last long!'

Aidan nodded. 'Just think how the ancient Britons managed. They would cross that in small, rudderless coracles. Many drowned, of course, but they tried constantly.'

They wheeled their horses and starting to walk back. Aidan began to pose his questions. 'Right, Let's see what you know. What is the fyrd?'

Wulfhere snapped his wits to attention. 'It is military service,' he began. 'All men, but usually only churls, can be called out when there is great danger. However, some churls give money dues instead of direct service to the king, depending upon their ages. A fighting churl is always free to leave one king and join the sign of another. If he does, though, he must relinquish everything he owns. It is a compromise between the churl's cherished freedom and the king's right to field an army.'

'In that case, where would the churl in question get his arms if he goes to another king?' Aidan shot at him.

'Then it is up to the new king to provide him with weapons, horses and the land rents or money. Certainly enough for the churl to make himself a new life with dignity. On death though, the actual weapons are revoked back to the king.'

'What about the land though?'

Wulfhere thought carefully. It was suddenly very important that he please his adopted brother with his answers. 'That might have to go back. It will all depend upon the churl's heir, and whether it was bocland or folcland. The first is held by a written title, but the latter by custom only.'

'Well,' Aidan drawled, 'it seems you did pay attention to your tutor's lessons after all. My Lord Burhred had his doubts! Next question. From where does any king get his money?'

Wulfhere knew that too. He had also listened to Penda whenever he had been given the opportunity. 'From royal estates or food rent paid in kind.'

Aidan was pleased and impressed. 'Any king rarely has to spend money paying or hiring men for building purposes. It's all down to our excellent class system, because every man knows exactly where he stands and whether he gives military service, food, or works for the king so many days a week. It's very good, but now tell me what you know about our wergild system.'

Wulfhere took time to collect his thoughts again. He was almost desperate to please. He was also enjoying this important, intellectual exercise.

'Wergild is the name that distinguishes one class from another in our society. It is also the price that a man must pay if he kills another outside warfare. The king is the most important man, so he has the highest wergild. Only that of another king can equal this. A member of the Gesith, like the late Lord Sihtric, would have a wergild of twelve hundred shillings if slain. Naturally, a slave has no wergild at all. These are the extremes of classes, and in between are the nobles and churls, whose wergild depends upon their class and position in society, from where they come and the merit of the king who holds their oath.'

'Excellent!' And Aidan beamed at him. 'Now what exactly is our oath?'

Wulfhere became very serious indeed. 'The oath of any man is the most precious possession he can own. That of a man with a high wergild is more valuable than that of someone lower in society.'

'Correct! But what about personal injuries, compensation and civil court matters?' Aidan persisted. He was rather amazed at just how much Wulfhere did know. Burhred was going to be even more startled. More of the late King Penda had rubbed off on this younger son than was realised.

'These are taken into account, according to the injury received and its gravity,' Wulfhere explained, then looked at his companion. 'What is your wergild?'

Aidan grinned. 'I am a four hundred shillings man, with seven hides of land, now operated by my sons. I still take half of the rents and profits, they have the rest. When I die, they take all divided between them.'

'What sort of land is it?' Wulfhere asked, very impressed.

Aidan shrugged: 'It's folcland. I've no written charter yet, though, I rather think Lord Burhred intends to do something about this for me while I'm here with you,' he explained dryly.

Wulfhere nodded sagely to himself. He had never thought deeply about all this; there had been no need. Now though, in his enforced isolation, with a long absence yawning ahead, he found he was deeply interested in all which concerned his people. He remembered when his father had held a court of justice and he wished now he had taken the time and trouble to attend more often. Peada had, of course, and he grimaced to himself. Only now did he fully appreciate why the Witan would never had voted him as their next king, with or without fighting. Peada had been the obvious choice, but, he vowed, my day will come.

Aidan stretched in the saddle. 'That's enough. I think you may know more than quite a few other kings right now. I'll race you back,' he challenged.

When they reached their camp, a delicious smell of roast pig greeted them. Aidan had killed a suckling that morning from a sounder of boar they had tracked and hunted.

Egwina served them after they had washed in the river. She put long slices of well-roasted meat and crackling on two large platters. She also gave a share to Alcium and Edith before retiring with her own food.

For the first time in ages—she could not really remember how long—Egwina had started to eat properly. The unexpected kindness touched her and had helped her to make up her mind. She knew her father would still be undergoing misery, and he must be rescued. When the men had finished eating they wiped their fingers fastidiously on a damp rabbit skin used for that purpose. She approached them nervously. Her lips had gone dry and fear filled her but she had to pluck up courage. It was impossible to continue like this.

Aidan and Wulfhere looked at her, then each other as they sat on the grass, to one side of the fire. 'Yes?' Aidan asked gruffly. He could see the girl was terrified of something and he frowned.

Wulfhere looked around carefully, but could not see any stranger or anyone from the big house. Alcium was outside his hut keeping a discreet eye upon them, while he laboured to saw timbers and build a proper home for himself and Edith.

Egwina was suddenly lost for words. Her throat had dried up so, without hesitating anymore, she lifted her tunic and pulled out a small pouch purse which had hung from a thong around her neck, and between her breasts. She opened a drawstring and held it, so they could both see dried vegetable contents.

Both men were puzzled and looked up at her with silent questions. Egwina took a deep breath and told them in a torrent of words.

'I'm supposed to put this poison in your food or, if I don't get that opportunity, to use the sword and kill you both at night if I can!'

Wulfhere and Aidan were speechless, and Egwina saw she had them both off balance. 'Cyneard hates you for being the reason his son is hostage. He hates you for buying his slaves against his will and then releasing them. He hates you because you're not afraid of him. He intends to see you both dead, one way or the other. He has been very cruel to me and I have had no redress because he holds my father as his hostage and treats him vilely. Please help me to free him and then protect

100

both of us.' Her voice broke and she burst into a storm of heart-rending tears.

CHAPTER SEVEN

The whole tun reeled with appalled shock. It was difficult for the people to understand, because murder was a rare crime with them. They relied on each other so much. It was incredible to think a man had died outside of warfare or a feud. It was a total blight on every family and people looked at each other, asking silent questions. Was it him? And why? Eanwulf was a respected elder even if he did have the misfortune of being a close friend of that opinionated, dogmatic, outspoken Lord Burhred.

The Northumbrian clerks went immediately on the alert and halted their mathematical calculations. There were three of them, now suddenly conscious they were quite alone among a multitude of hostile Mercians. It was true not one hand or weapon had even been half-lifted against them but they were most conscious of narrowed eyes that followed their every move.

Burhred's shock was the greatest of all, and Oswald became increasingly concerned about his mental welfare. The elder with Oscar and Ealstan, plus a handful of others, had followed

Elfrida back to view the body. Then they collected it and lovingly brought it back with them.

Burhred retired to his home for two days and two nights, only grunting when addressed as he sat in a corner of his large room. He ate what was necessary to keep his body functioning, but appeared not to know what the food was. Oswald, although appalled himself, realised Burhred could not go on like this.

King Peada, escorted by his gesith, had called and wasted his time. Burhred simply refused to see him and Oswald had to invent a hasty excuse for such rudeness. Elfrida visited. She was still in a form of shock and affected by Burhred's unusual behaviour.

On the third morning Burhred came back to them and gestured to Oswald. 'Get that girl back and Ealstan. We will talk,' he grunted and changed his clothing in which he had sat and brooded for the whole two days. 'We will talk in private, just the four of us. So get rid of the slaves somewhere!' he ordered brusquely in a tone that made Oswald's eyebrows elevate.

Elfrida was nervous at the little gathering. She knew Ealstan, but not as a person, and it was easy to see he was still in his own form of shock. Between Eanwulf and Ealstan had been a long friendship, even though they sparked each other up now and again.

When they were all together and safely

102

alone, with the door firmly shut and latched, Burhred surveyed them in turn. They all waited for him to speak as their natural leader.

'I am angry,' he started, 'but I think I understand some of it, though the killer is still beyond me,' and he turned to Elfrida. 'Remember how you found him?'

Elfrida nodded and gulped. It was hardly likely she would ever forget. It was not that she hadn't seen a body before, they all had, but it was the manner of the death that stuck in her mind.

'Think back to how Eanwulf was dressed,' Burhred ordered, and they did. He let a few moments pass for reflection, then brought out his next point. 'When a person rides, he acquires his own stamp and style in the saddle. Eanwulf and myself, although not of the same build, did have a similar stance. I know people have commented upon this in the past.'

Elfrida was the first to understand. 'And he was wearing the same coloured clothing the day he died, as you. That spear was meant for you! Eanwulf died as a result of mistaken identity!'

Burhred flashed her a look. He might have known she would guess first. 'Exactly!'

Oswald spoke next this time ahead of Elfrida. 'But why out there alone?'

Burhred turned to him. 'The message! Someone had sent a message to me, expecting me to come and I bet Eanwulf was asked to pass this on, but did not. He was probably trying to help and thought he'd save me a trip.'

'And he died instead of you!' Ealstan finished heavily.

Then it was Elfrida's turn. 'From the rear, the spear thrower would easily mistake him for you!'

'And Eanwulf would suspect nothing at all. He would have known the person who sent the message and had ridden forward in all innocence,' Oswald added.

Ealstan paused. His heart was so heavy. 'Then that lets out those Northumbrian clerks to start with,' he pointed out. 'They have nothing to gain by murder, because they are the victors. This place is theirs anyhow. And they would hardly go riding around, alone, in what they know was hostile territory.'

Burhred nodded. 'That's how I worked it out,' he paused, thinking back. 'It will be common knowledge that not everyone is enthusiastic about King Peada so I suppose we could say there is a question mark over the whole of the Witan.'

Elfrida chipped in. 'It also means you are still a target, sir!'

'By all the gods, she is right!' Oswald gasped.

Ealstan's mind worked in another direction. 'I doubt it's anyone from the Witan, because they are all getting on in years. And many of them will not have thrown a spear in a long

104

time. We all know, it is a weapon that needs considerable skill to use with such accuracy. That spear was also embedded quite deeply!'

Burhred nodded again. 'That is also true but it is possible, even in these modern times, to hire a mercenary to do the dirty work for someone. A rapid payment of appropriate coinage, at a secret location, directly after the murder, and the mercenary could now be many a mile away. Money always talks!'

'Where do we start to look?' Elfrida asked. This was all quite beyond her. It was like looking for one solitary flea in the fetid winter floor rushes. An impossible task.

Oswald's mind had moved on to another tack. 'It means Burhred, you can go nowhere alone now,' he said forcefully. 'Such a failure, when the dust does settle, means a second try!'

This was a conclusion Burhred had also reached and it stuck in his throat. 'Maybe, and maybe not,' he answered enigmatically. He dived to one side where there were a pile of papers, made from grasses, pulped wood, and old rags: a trade given to the slaves. It was a laborious process to make something for writing, and the finished objects were always highly valuable. Burhred picked up a sheet, covered with his delicate runic script, and he waved it under their noses. 'Here!' he stated a little ponderously. 'This is what I've been doing in between thinking since Eanwulf died.

'I'm going to stand before the king and the

Witan,' he told them. 'I'm going to let them know I have written everything down and, if I should die prematurely through foul means, I have arranged for all of them to go to King Oswiu and charge him to investigate. We can all be sure, the Northumbrian clerks will see that is done. Whether I like that king or not is irrelevant. What I do know is, he is one of these ardent Christians, and a very religious man. He will not tolerate something so foul as murder on his newly acquired territory. When I finish speaking my piece before everyone, including the Northumbrian clerks, these papers will vanish for safekeeping!'

'Where?' Oswald asked practically.

Burhred pondered. It was a very good question. 'I'll wrap them in waterproofs and . . . ' He halted, brow furrowed. Where was a good place? Down with Wulfhere? Who could take them? If Oswald disappeared by himself, this would be noted, and his gaze rested on Elfrida. She was used to slipping off by herself. No one would question her vanishing yet again. Everyone's eyes rested speculatively upon her, and Elfrida knew she had started to blush.

'Perfect!' Oswald guessed. 'And the sooner the better.'

Burhred echoed that sentiment. He grimaced to himself. It was only a short while ago he had wondered if he had allowed for all possible contingencies, especially the unexpected. This was a matter that had never crossed his mind. He had often wondered when a matter was debated if there would be a risk to a man who opposed a specific motion. Now he knew but that Eanwulf should die in his place had never entered his head.

Elfrida felt her heart start to pump with anticipation. For the first time since discovering Eanwulf's body, her spirits lifted. Perhaps she might have a chance to see Wulfhere in the not too distant future. With an effort, she struggled to keep her features impassive but Burhred saw through her.

This was exactly what she wanted and he cursed to himself, ran over all other possibilities and realised there were none. 'You'll go with Oswald, of course,' he told her with a bland expression. Meaning, you will have no chance to be alone with Wulfhere.

'Oh no!' Oswald objected. 'I'm not leaving you alone here now!'

Burhred turned and scowled at him. Oswald did not know where Elfrida's heart lay and he could hardly tell him now. Yet he must be informed sometime. 'You'll go and see about the adoption and make it formal and public,' he ordered, thinking fast on his feet now. 'Then you can say you are going away with her for a few days to get to know each other properly. And nothing will happen in your absence. The killer will never dare strike again so soon. It would make it all too obvious.

Right now, he is in a funk of a state because he knows he killed the wrong man, and the whole of this place is in turmoil. The fact that King Peada actually came here and I did not see him speaks volumes!'

Oswald, thought about this: it made sense, but he did not like it one bit. He opened his mouth to remonstrate, but caught the tiny shake from Burhred, and his frown. He was up to something again, although Oswald had no idea what this could be.

Burhred was in turmoil inside. He was over the shock of Eanwulf's death, which deeply grieved him. He had been a good man and had not deserved such an ending, yet, wrack his brains as he might, he could not fathom out who the killer might be. Even with their battle losses the tun still held many people, most of whom he knew, and it was inconceivable one was a murderer. Deep in his heart he knew it was possible. The killer might never be found, especially a mercenary, if used, which now seemed likely. An investigation would be filled with difficulties. The king, the elders, and even those Northumbrian clerks would try, but he doubted whether any positive evidence would ever be produced. The whole thing reflected very badly on King Peada because he showed he did not wholly control his area, which made a bad debut point. The snag was, with this kind of event, Northumbria might decide to station soldiers here, which was the last thing Burhred wanted.

Ealstan had been silent. 'Is it at all possible, someone was out hunting, saw Eanwulf's movements, thought he was game, and he was killed accidentally?'

They all considered this, Burhred very impatiently, Oswald uncertainly. Elfrida doubtfully.

'It's possible,' Oswald said finally, 'but unlikely. There's not much game in this area, until one gets among the trees. Only the wolf pack might be around at this time of year, and they can make enough noise to awaken the dead when they start to howl,' he said and flinched at his unfortunate choice of words.

It did flit across Elfrida's mind to wonder about her brother. He was a fair hunter, and nothing delighted him more than returning with fresh game. She kept this thought to herself but she did wonder where he might have been. Messing about with Alicia, hopefully? At this rate, he would make her pregnant and have to marry her in a hurry, unless that was Alicia's plan to snare him. She was as cunning and deadly as a snake to get what she wanted.

'Stop daydreaming, girl!' Burhred snapped at her suddenly. 'I just addressed you. What do you think?'

Elfrida felt herself blush again. She had not heard a word, and Burhred knew this perfectly well. He was annoyed afresh. He knew she had been daydreaming about Wulfhere.

'Are you ready to go with Oswald for this adoption, which *you* want?'

She looked nervously at Oswald and wondered what he thought about it deep down. Did he feel as if he was being stampeded into something against his will? Then she saw him smile. He had a generous, warm smile, and his eyes were kind, as they held hers.

'Let's go right now!' Oswald said firmly, and nodded towards the door. She sprang up, opened it and they went out together. Burhred watched them and shook his head. 'It's all a very bad business—except that.'

'Any of your bright ideas?' Ealstan asked.

Burhred shook his head firmly. 'Not one!' he admitted. 'And that is something that really bothers me!' He paused: 'Right now, I don't think I'm sure of anything except our man must stay hidden and for quite a while. Those papers go down to him and Aidan for safekeeping!' he said angrily.

Ealstan turned it all over in his mind. 'I think it would be prudent to let Wulfhere know everything that happens here in case Aidan is sick or even dies. I know you call him a young man, but he is not really. It is true he is only in his thirties but he has had a hard life fighting. Battles wear out a body, remember. There is one thing you could do which would upset everything nicely!'

Burhred looked at him with interest. Ealstan coming out with a bright idea? He waited expectantly.

'Tell the king outright you suspect him and Northumbria!'

Burhred gave a wolfish grin. 'For once, you are a step ahead of me,' he praised. 'It would certainly put the onus very heavily on the king to find the murderer—if he could! At the same time it just about guarantees I can carry on breathing. Excellent, old friend!' and he stood and stretched. 'Coming?'

'My pleasure!' Ealstan replied with a throaty chuckle, and together they sauntered over to where the king and the elders listened to Oswald, and Elfrida.

They had both presented a reasonable argument in a logical manner, which appealed to anyone with an orderly mind. To one side stood Cynewulf and Alicia, and King Peada flashed them both a look. The king took pride in his position and, with his matrimonial connection, knew more about the Northumbrian king than any of his people. He had been totally opposed to the battle at Loidis from the very start. There had been many instances, in his opinion, when his father showed exactly from where Wulfhere had inherited his temper. There was no doubt it was providential Wulfhere had been killed. At least his youngest brother could be moulded to conform with Peada's own ideas which were

111

totally pacific.

He knew he was not a strong man like his father but neither did he consider himself weak. What he failed to understand was the impossibility of hunting with the hounds as well as running as the game. This made him very indecisive, and in such situations he was inclined to take the easy way out.

He liked Cynewulf and Alicia. They were the up-and-coming generation of Mercians who would adapt beautifully. Now he felt a flash of annoyance, because, quite suddenly Cynewulf spoke, almost interrupting him.

'I object, sire!' Cynewulf began a little pompously. 'I'm the only male in the family now and I consider I have the right to plan my sister's status, especially now,' he said, meaning since Mercia's defeat.

Elfrida did not make the mistake of turning towards her brother, or even addressing him. She kept her eyes fixed firmly on the king with what she hoped was an appealing look. 'I wish to take my time, sire. My brother has our family home. I just wish for my legal half share, which I shall give to my adoptive father for safekeeping. Also, in our culture, males and females are equal.'

The king knew it was a very valid point. He knew little about Oswald, except that he was friends and lived with a testy elder who, quite frankly, terrified him. He had known Burhred all his life and had always felt very uncomfortable around him, yet his late father had thought the world of him. From his eye corner, he saw that the elder had appeared and was waiting to speak to him. This he did not fancy at all.

'I see no objection to this adoption,' and he glanced at his Witan who nodded almost en masse. Naturally, in such a matter they all followed his lead. The only ones missing were the murdered man, Eanwulf, his close friend Ealstan and the dreaded Lord Burhred, a twelve-hundred-shilling man. Now the latter two stood together and King Peada felt a wild flutter of anxiety. He half-waved a hand in agreement and dismissal.

Cynewulf went to scowl and felt Alicia's fingers jab him in the middle of the back. You fool, she thought, don't upset a king when you want favours of rank in the future. There were times when she almost despaired of Cynewulf. Indeed, during the last couple of days, she had allowed her eyes to drift speculatively towards the Northumbrian clerks. Was she throwing the incorrect dice in her gamble?

Cynewulf realised his crass error, hastily bowed his head and backed away, flinching at the cold look in Alicia's eyes. He was very much in awe of her mind, which, at times, was too devious for him. He was not a bad young man, simply rather foolish and far too flattered by Alicia's apparent devotion.

'What made you speak like that? You upset

the king, and he'll never make you a noble. Then where will we be? We are just ordinary churls because you have not proved yourself in battle, and that is all finished and done with now!' she hissed with annoyance.

Cynewulf looked at her miserably. 'I didn't think!' he admitted and flushed. 'My sister always gets everyone running after her, it makes me sick!'

Alicia snorted. 'Don't bother your head about her. She is a nobody, without even one close friend!'

Burhred watched the couple walk away and ducked his head to King Peada and stared at him steadily with hooded eyes. King Peada broke eye contact first. Satisfied, he had enforced his strong personality upon the king, Burhred turned his attention to the others of the Witan. Men he had known all his life, some good, some weak, a couple who were doubtful, but surely not a killer among them? As his eyes went from face to face he felt smug satisfaction when they all looked away from him.

'Sire!' he said, turning back to the king now he had total attention. 'My friend has been murdered. A deed most strange!'

Peada jerked to sharp attention. Since when had murder been described so mildly. 'What do you mean?' he asked uncertainly. This man's wisdom was well renowned, and he disliked him very much without being able to say specifically why.

'Eanwulf's murder was a gross mistake. That spear was meant for me!' Burhred announced flatly, and now he did have everyone's immediate attention. Slowly, taking his time, selecting each word with precision, he spoke aloud his suspicions.

Peada went stiff as he listened. The story had the ring of truth, yet one point worried him. 'Why did you not speak up for me to be king?' he asked with curiosity and hurt. Peada was one of those people who would love to be loved, and cannot understand otherwise.

Burhred never hesitated; neither did he wrap up his words. 'I did not think you are the best man, sire!'

The Witan stilled with horror, and the king's eyes opened wide. 'But why not?' he blurted.

It was well-known Lord Burhred was no sycophant, he never had been; it was against his nature and temperament.

'Youth!' Burhred drawled. 'Inexperience!' he added. 'And too much love for Northumbria!' he spat harshly.

Many people had now gathered out of interest, and there were many gasps and even the king was taken aback. An angry flush reddened his cheeks. He opened his mouth to remonstrate harshly, then became aware of the crowd gathered around, listening with great interest. Among them were the Northumbrian clerks. He bit back hot words and forced himself to be his usual affable man but he writhed inside. Burhred had not changed at all. He needed an elder like this as much as he needed a hole in his head.

Burhred found him pathetically easy to read so he continued with a straight face. 'Because of what has happened I have taken certain precautions. All details of this disgusting event have been written down, and if anything should happen to me or mine, my specific instructions are that my writing is to go to King Oswiu in person.' He halted to let the words sink in before continuing, his eyes harsh upon those of the king. 'And it is useless any person trying to get into my house to look for them as my slaves are fully alert and they have been told to knife anyone night or day. They will do it as well because I look after my slaves,' he said smoothly, and everyone knew this was the absolute truth. Burhred also planned to manumit some of them to ensure total loyalty but this he did not bother to explain.

'I'm sorry you have so little faith in me!' Peada managed to get out gently, which was the truth.

Burhred decided it was time to relax the king a little. 'We all have to learn through practice. And I am sure you are anxious to do the best you can for all of your people!'

Peada grabbed the straw quicker than a drowning man. 'Of course! Of course!'

116

Burhred had said all that which was necessary. Now was the time to go, and let the king sweat it out a bit.

He turned on his heels and, with Ealstan following, walked away with dignity. Once inside his home with his companions, he turned to Oswald.

'You two clear off in the morning at dawn. I will be perfectly safe here now. Even those Northumbrian clerks will be concerned about my welfare!' and he smiled wryly. Deep down in his heart, he knew that Eanwulf would thoroughly approve the precautions he had taken.

CHAPTER EIGHT

'What sword?' Aidan and Wulfhere asked in unison.

Egwina cringed at the tone of their voices. What she had started, she must finish. It was all or nothing now.

'My father's sword. It's in that long bundle, which I brought with me. Lord Cyneard made me under threat!'

Wulfhere frowned. 'Your father?' he prodded.

Egwina turned to him with relief. His eyes were curt, but not hostile like those of his older brother. She sensed he might be the

117

more receptive of the two. From long reticence, sullenness and fear, she suddenly found her tongue and her words poured out like a long released dam.

'We are freeborn,' she started to explain carefully. They must believe her and help. 'My father was lord of our small manor and it was a proper little manor too, not like that place over there!' and she nodded, in the general direction of Cyneard's home. 'We were such a happy little family too.' She halted for a few seconds, thinking back, remembering all that had gone forever.

'Go on!' Wulfhere encouraged, fascinated now. 'What happened?'

'My father went to battle for our local king, was wounded and taken prisoner. Just about then, my mother died in childbed, so there was only me left. My father did manage to escape and came for me but I slowed him down. I wasn't used to much riding,' she explained, and shook her head chagrined. 'We were recaptured, and there was no point in holding us for ransom, because the estate and all father owned had gone. We were sceataless, no coins at all. Because we were such a small family there was no one interested enough to pay ransom. We ended up being sold into slavery together. I suppose, in a way, we were lucky that Cyneard bought us as a pair. We could so easily have been separated. He bought my father's sword to wear himself,

118

though he is not entitled to that weapon. He had to pay a lot of money for the sword, of course. He is a cruel man. His wife is terrified of him, as is his little daughter. Even his son is afraid, and he only holds his retainers because he happens to be bigger than most of them, and a better fighter. If there were another lord in the region I know the free men would leave and give their oath elsewhere. He raped me and used me as a means of revenge for losing his son as hostage. It's not that he loves his son. Cyneard only really loves himself. His son was just another possession, like I am as a slave.'

Aidan nodded. All of this made sense in their society, and it was obvious the girl told the truth. The tears in her eyes were not faked.

Wulfhere's heart went out to her. From his disliking her so much, not knowing what she had endured, he now felt attraction. Once cleaned up, she was a different person. Although not beautiful as the word was understood, she did have a certain allure. He was fascinated with her story and flashed a look at his companion to see his reaction.

'How many here know your whole story?' Aidan asked.

Egwina hesitated, uncertainly. 'I'm not sure. I think most of them know my background, but without the details. Certainly no one dares to question Cyneard, not even his retainers. The only man he talks to or drinks with is Raebald.

He is the one who kept riding over here to see what you were doing all the time, especially with Edith and Alcium. He is mean as well.'

Wulfhere felt manliness rise. 'I would be pleased to take those two swine out,' he stated flatly and threw Aidan a challenging look.

The churl returned it, eyebrows lifted questioningly. It was not a bad idea at all. Wulfhere had to have his first problem fight, and his first kill, but was he ready yet to tangle with an older, more experienced man? Perhaps that might be pushing luck too far but this was not something he could say before the girl.

'We will talk about what can be done,' Aidan replied soothingly, 'and then we'll have another talk among the three of us.'

Egwina bit her lip. This had gone far better that she had dared to hope but now there was another problem.

'When I last went over for herbs he grabbed me, hit me a number of times round the face and said if you were both still alive by the time of the next new moon my father will be dead!'

'Is that so?' Aidan drawled. He thought rapidly. 'That gives us about three weeks,' and he nodded sagely to himself. He turned back to the girl. 'I know it's very easy for me to say, words can be so trite, but carry on as you've been doing these three weeks. It will give me time to work out a decent plan and put it into action.'

With that Egwina turned away, satisfied, a weight lifted from her shoulders. To start with, the older brother had terrified her. Anyone who could put Cyneard into fear had to be someone worthwhile and hope soared. What could possibly happen if Cyneard was killed was something about which she had no intention of thinking. It was a case of living each day as it came.

'I will kill the swine, release her father and he can then become lord of the manor here,' Wulfhere said carefully and hoped Aidan would approve.

Aidan took a deep breath. This was all fairly logical, except for one point that had obviously escaped Wulfhere's attention. 'You do that and the news might spread far and wide when Lord Burhred wants your very existence kept quiet. Not just your safety, but for Mercia!' he pointed out coolly.

Wulfhere flushed. 'Oh!' was all he managed to get out.

Aidan watched the emotions chase across his face. 'We will work something out but it will be in a more subtle manner!'

He thought a moment. 'The thing to do is to provoke him into challenging you!' he advised cunningly. 'Then, when you win, the spoils are automatically yours to do with as you choose!'

Wulfhere brightened. 'Splendid!' Then looking sideways, he saw movement. 'Riders coming!'

Aidan was startled. He had let his guard slip, for once. 'Who the hell is it now?'

They both stared hard, then sprang to their feet. 'That is Oswald. My Lord Burhred's companion. And that's a girl with him. I think her name is—' and he racked his brains. 'That's it! It is Elfrida, though I know very little about her!'

Aidan was alarmed. He felt a sudden unease. They strolled over and waited for Oswald and Elfrida to dismount. Alcium ran over to take their horses, and the four Mercians looked at each other. Oswald gave Aidan a hard stare of warning. Elfrida let her eyes rest on Wulfhere, though she was suddenly very conscious of another young female nearby. Quite a pretty one too and her heart gave a little lurch of dismay. She furrowed her brow. The girl puzzled her. She was dressed like a slave, yet now she turned and stared frankly at the unexpected guests. A well broken-in slave would have behaved in a more servile manner, not stared over appraisingly. Elfrida felt a sudden confusion and total disappointment. What exactly she had expected to find was certainly not this—a quite attractive girl, of her own age group, who did not appear to be in the slightest bit in awe of wonderful Wulfhere. Quite suddenly, her world collapsed.

Aidan strode forward to greet Oswald, with Wulfhere at his side. Oswald paused a second to look around. He frowned, perplexed. There was a man and woman to one side, a young quite pretty girl on the other and he was confused.

'What's going on here with all these people?' and he gestured with one hand. 'You two are supposed to be quite alone!'

Aidan spoke for both of them. 'There have had to be some alterations, and now we have a bit of a problem to deal with, but nothing I can't manage. More to the point, what are you doing here so soon and who is that girl with you? We were supposed to be left alone for quite a while. Has Lord Burhred sent you?'

Oswald gave a heavy sigh. 'He certainly has. The girl is my adopted daughter and she will be coming here from now on as the courier. She is perfectly capable. I have bad news of home. Murder!' he said bluntly.

Aidan and Wulfhere walked to one side, where the three of them could sit on a slight slope. Oswald then brought them up to date with homely events.

'It's been a very bad business indeed. There is no doubt that the spear was meant for Burhred, but who threw it we have no idea. As you can no doubt imagine, the place has been in an uproar. The old men of the Witan are useless, and King Peada not much better. We are pretty certain it was not the doing of the Northumbrian clerks, because they are quite motiveless.'

123

Aidan and Wulfhere were deeply shocked, hardly able to take in this information. Wulfhere noted the strange girl sat next to Oswald, very quiet, almost withdrawn. He gave her a quick scrutiny, then turned his attention back to Oswald who now went into more detail.

Elfrida sat as if frozen. He had given her a quick look, and that was all. Who was the other girl and what was she doing here? She itched to ask her own questions, but had sense enough to keep her mouth shut.

Oswald paused for a moment, 'I have a gut feeling we might never find out who the killer is. Especially if a mercenary was used. As for motive, we can only presume someone objected to Burhred's stance against Peada. Burhred's later speech to the king and the elders must also have thrown everybody. Especially Burhred's threat that his paper would go to King Oswiu if anything else happened. King Oswiu would turn our tun upside down to find the guilty person, which is something beyond Peada. Daughter, the paper!'

Elfrida blushed a little, then slipped her hand underneath her tunic to where the precious evidence had been hidden, between her breasts, supported by a cord. She flashed a look at Wulfhere; was he noticing? Was he even interested? But Wulfhere was too stunned at Oswald's revelations. He felt

124

choked inside. Eanwulf with his friend Ealstan had been on his side with Burhred, and some swine had wiped him out without giving him a chance. Guilt descended as, for the first time, he understood fully what some people, a mere handful, were prepared to do for—him. He swallowed heavily and felt a lump in his throat as this news humbled him. He then made a personal vow to himself. No matter what trials and tribulations the future might throw at him, he would strive to be the best man Mercia had ever had and be the best king possible. The onus of responsibility was awesome, and he could only pray to all the gods he was up to the task. Then his head reminded his heart he must make himself very worthy. A good man was dead. How many others were destined to follow—because of him? His past behaviour made him quiver with shame. How callow, selfish and arrogant he had been. He knew his cheeks flushed with personal embarrassment as he castigated himself savagely.

Elfrida kept throwing peeps at him. Wulfhere sat on the grass, arms around his knees, head lowered, eyes staring at the ground, obviously seeing nothing but dreadful past memories. Her heart went out to him. If only he would look at her, she would smile, and with her eyes tell him it would be all right one day. Her love for him was so much. It was nothing but physical pain. She sat quite mute and looked over at the other girl, who was busying herself with a cauldron in which bubbled meat, and from which came a tantalising odour.

She took a look at the other couple. They did have the look of slaves about them except their heads were held high, and their dress was superior to that of one in a servile position. Were they free people? If so, what were they doing here? The man certainly walked tall and proud, and the woman, perhaps his wife, copied him. The pretty young girl had been talking to them. Now she came back and busied herself again with the food. She simply had to be a slave. So why was she so familiar with the couple? It was all a puzzle, quite beyond her.

She turned and saw that Wulfhere was looking at her. 'Who are they?' she asked, nodding at the couple.

Aidan, still in deep conversation with Oswald and Wulfhere, realised his manners had not been the best to this girl who had, after all, ridden here with Burhred's precious paper hidden on her person.

'They were slaves, but we bought them and freed them. They are two extra pairs of eyes for us, and both Mercian,' and he explained the situation. Elfrida was fascinated. Wulfhere now took the time to study her a little. She was not bad-looking, if one liked that type, but she could not compare to Egwina he was amazed to acknowledge. Now the girl had been cleaned up and dressed better, she was quite attractive. He also realised she had backbone as her story proved. The misery she had undergone, the vile rape: Egwina knew more about life's badness than he knew existed. She too humbled him. What a soft, easy life of luxury had been his before Aidan came into it.

He made a rapid comparison between the lives of these two girls. In many ways, the girl from his tun had led a life not totally dissimilar to his. She had always been well fed and clothed, tutored and cosseted, with no idea what real suffering was. Who did at his tun, he asked himself with unusual honesty? To some extent, they were just about all degenerate, so was it any great surprise the Northumbrians had defeated Mercia at Loidis? He made another vow to himself. When he did become king he would make sure, very sure indeed, that the fighting warriors were always kept fit, ready and alert. There was a lot to be said for the way the old Romans trained their legions.

Wulfhere watched Aidan and Oswald stroll off together in deep conversation. He itched to know what they were saying, because he guessed it was about him. Oswald would be taking back a progress report to Burhred. Wulfhere gave a little swallow of embarrassment, and just hoped it would be a good one.

He felt like a walk himself, there was so much on his mind, but it would be the height of bad manners to leave the girl alone when she had ridden to help him. 'Care for a stroll?' he asked casually.

Elfrida beamed at him and they walked off in the opposite direction to that of the two men, both acutely aware of the other but for very different reasons. Elfrida's heart had lifted, while that of Wulfhere had sunk. What was Aidan saying about him? He fell sharply nervous and realised he was walking automatically, ignoring the girl at his side.

Elfrida wondered what was wrong with him. He had not always been so dumb, quite the reverse. What was wrong with her that she could not engender even a little reaction? Now it was the turn of her heart to fall. She wished she had not come now. Oswald was perfectly capable of delivering Burhred's paper himself, and it suddenly hit her, that perhaps this was just a trial run. Was she going to have to do this by herself in the future? It had all started out so wonderfully well and now was going horribly wrong.

Oswald had led her in a circuitous route, constantly checking their back trail, but no one had attempted to follow. They had not hurried, but cold-camped out for two nights, talking gently, getting to know each other. Oswald was the type of company she did enjoy. He was never garrulous, but very entertaining, dryly relating tales of years ago, when he and Burhred had been young men. Her heart warmed to him and she knew he was going to make a wonderful adopted father.

She flashed another look at Wulfhere. Why didn't he talk to her? What was the point of this aimless perambulation? It was not as if he was shy and had only just met her. It had to be that gorgeous-looking girl, and the knife of jealousy entered her heart. Her emotions see-sawed violently, and she was ready to hate the slave girl which was, she reminded herself, stupid, because a slave was a nobody.

Then Aidan turned and beckoned. They trotted over, Wulfhere glad to be included in men's talk again. He had felt distinctly uncomfortable with this girl Elfrida who had kept looking at him as if she half-expected him to come out with some worthy pronouncement.

'We'll talk inside now,' Aidan stated firmly. 'This important paper is in a waterproof, and we will bury it under one of the floorboards,' he explained as he led them back into the place where he and Wulfhere lived. 'Now you can hear what has been going on here!'

Elfrida and Oswald listened intently. So the girl was noble! She would obviously consider herself superior in rank to Wulfhere who, after all, was here in disguise as . . . the humble young brother Hoel. She bit her lip anxiously, which was not lost on Oswald. His heart went out to her, because on their ride down here, she had confided in him. Frankly, he thought

129

she was mad. Wulfhere as a son-in-law was the last person he would wish to know—unless he had altered drastically. Certainly Aidan had given an excellent report, which would please Burhred enormously. Oswald himself was very impressed, and one assessing look at young Wulfhere had shown another difference. He had filled out incredibly fast, and Oswald had a pretty shrewd idea how the young man had been worked to develop muscle so quickly. He also had a different attitude. All the brash cockiness had been knocked out of him. He was more respectful, even quieter and controlled—quite a pleasant person when compared to the youth of the past. A totally different Wulfhere indeed.

'I don't like any of this,' Oswald replied thoughtfully. 'You are supposed to keep a low profile. I don't think Lord Burhred would approve at all!'

Aidan threw him a wolfish leer, then began to speak rapidly. Oswald listened carefully, as a grin slid over his face. 'It could work. It has to, otherwise you might as well sound a horn, which will let everybody know Wulfhere is alive and thriving!' and he considered carefully, then nodded sagely.

Aidan explained a little more. 'Wulfhere has to be blooded some time, and this is as good an opportunity as any which might arise. If it all goes to plan, we will also have extra eyes and ears keeping vigilance for us down here,' he pointed out smoothly. 'During the next three weeks I'm going to perfect his weapons' skill, and he will be so exhausted each night that hopping into bed with anyone will be quite beyond him!'

Oswald bellowed a coarse laugh of amusement, then he became serious again. 'How many men can he arm, do you know?'

'Not yet but I intend to pump the girl dry. She'll cooperate because it is all to her benefit and she hates Cyneard. Who wouldn't after what we heard?'

Oswald hesitated a moment. 'What if he—?'

'In that case, I will have failed in my duty of making a king. Trust me! The material on which I have been working has proved far superior far to that which I envisaged. I predict he will turn out even better than Penda!' he said with confidence.

Later on, Oswald explained everything to Elfrida, and she listened with a sinking heart. She had ridden down here full of anticipation and hope and now these were dashed. It did cross her mind to speak bluntly to her adoptive father but instinct stayed her tongue. She knew what Lord Burhred would have to say and imagined his scorn. Nothing would be allowed to stand in the way of Mercia breaking free from Northumbria. Wulfhere was the people's only genuine hope though they did not know this yet.

Oswald was blissfully unaware of her

torment, and much too worried about the situation he had so unexpectedly found. He was acutely aware they dare not stay away from the tun too long, because this would be bound to arouse unfavourable comment. He guessed that Burhred would have Elfrida ride down here alone when messages had to be passed in the future. She was a natural loner. Deep down, he was appalled at the contingencies that had arisen. On top of Eanwulf's murder the situation in general might be considered bleak except that Aidan was as crafty at planning as Burhred.

'We will leave at dawn, daughter!' Oswald told her firmly. The sooner Burhred had these facts, the better.

Wulfhere was also deeply disturbed. King Penda had dealt with everything under the sun but never murder.

A point occurred to Aidan. 'Cyneard's son. Where did you take him? Far away?'

'He is not all that far away. One long day's ride with a couple of woodsmen whom I happen to know very well, a man and wife. I have a suspicion, after what you said about Cyneard, the boy might even be pleased to get away from his father. You ride east for ten miles, then north for six and you'll come to their cottage. Impossible to miss. Not many people go in that direction, so my tracks will still show.'

'How did you get him out?' Wulfhere asked

curiously.

'Myself and the woodsman came, ostensibly to sell goods, then we simply grabbed the boy when he came into the hall with his father. Shoved a knife against his throat and hauled him out. There was nothing Cyneard could do with a knife at the boy's throat. We were on our horses in a flash, theirs weren't even saddled. Obviously, they sent trackers after us but, with all the woodsman knew, we went here and there until I was completely lost. The boy only struggled for a bit, then relaxed and almost seemed to enjoy himself. The only tears he shed were for his mother and sister. It was all incredibly simple.'

Aidan nodded. Trust Oswald to run such a smooth operation. Once Cyneard and Raebald had been dealt with it would not be at all difficult to return the boy to his mother.

Wulfhere's mind had been moving in a different direction. 'I'm worried about Lord Burhred,' he stated bluntly. 'I know he's taken all these precautions, but I would rather him be alive than dead. All for my sake,' he murmured in a low voice. 'It all seems so wrong to me!' His lip twisted scornfully as he thought about his elder brother, King Peada. All he would really do would be to talk and waffle. In Wulfhere's eyes, Peada was the original non-action man. If only he could return right now and make a fighting challenge for the kingship but, having had only such a short time with Aidan, he acknowledged he was not quite ready. The coming fight with Cyneard was going to be of critical importance. After that took place, he must develop himself even more: strengthen muscles that had already appeared until he was rock-hard like Aidan. He was sharp enough to realise the coming fight with Cyneard was going to be more than a rescue operation for two people. It would also be his baptism.

Elfrida felt acute jealousy for Egwina and realised there was nothing she could do about it. How glib and silly she had been telling Burhred she was happy to ride out alone. She now realised she'd be expected to do this as and when Burhred dictated, and again there was nothing she could do. She knew if she complained or objected, the elder would not hesitate to remind her of her duty to Mercia as a whole and Burhred's tongue could be so caustic; Elfrida knew that was one argument she could never win.

They rode off early, when dawn was only just breaking so no one from Cyneard's house saw their departure. Aidan had also advised them not to ride direct, but in a large, confusing circle. Aidan and Wulfhere watched their departure with very mixed feelings.

'Right!' Aidan snapped suddenly. 'Back to work!' he barked. 'I want you expert with the sword and dagger before we move onto the next stage of our plan.'

'Do we have one?' Wulfhere asked himself.

'And you, girl, go about your work as normal then, this evening. I shall wish to question you about Cyneard's and who will be in there. I shall want a full detailed picture!' Aidan told Egwina and she understood. They were only two and she gave a little gulp of anxiety. So much depended upon these two men. Was she asking too much of them?

Later that evening, when they had eaten, the three of them sat outside and Aidan started his questions, while Wulfhere listened intently.

'How many fighting males does Cyneard have?'

Egwina paid attention and counted carefully. 'Six, which include Raebald, but I don't know how good the rest of them are. You see, five of them are only armed slaves on the promise of their freedom if they serve Cyneard properly for ten years.'

Aidan thought about that. Any man with freedom dangled before his eyes could make a very difficult enemy even if ten years was a long time to wait. On the other hand, if they could be made to switch sides they could be very useful indeed.

'Raebald—what exactly is his position?'

Egwina hesitated. 'I am not sure, but I think he is some kind of relation, a distant cousin. From the little bits, I overheard he had trouble

135

at home with his father and set off to make his own way in life.'

'Describe him!'

Egwina could certainly do that. 'He is as bad-tempered as Cyneard, and every bit as brutal. He also raped me. I pretended I was sick, but that made no difference. I should imagine he is furious that I was sent down here, but I think he is a bit afraid of Cyneard. I did hear them argue a few times, but Raebald always backed down first. He likes his drink, and so does Cyneard, and neither of them will be as fit and strong as you two brothers.'

'Where does everyone sleep?'

Egwina answered, relaxing a little. Perhaps this older churl was not so fearsome after all. His brusqueness was simply his way. 'There are numerous cubicles for the family along the left side of the hall, which is not very big,' and she twitched her nose elegantly. 'It's only a miniscule manor house. The slaves and other men sleep outside. There are hounds, though, but if I come with you they won't give a problem, because they all know me.'

'Excellent!'

'And your father?' Wulfhere asked gently, deciding to let the girl know he was not just a puppet.

Egwina turned to him. 'He has also been kept with the outside slaves,' she explained with a catch in her voice. How had he been treated since she had been serving the brothers? Whenever she went over for her herbs she had tried to peep at him, to no avail.

Aidan nodded more to himself than the other two. 'We can ride the short distance, then leave the horses hobbled and approach on foot. We two will stay hidden while you attract the sentry's attention, and I will then take him out. We enter as noiselessly as possible, and go straight into the hall—!'

'And I'll storm into Cyneard's cubicle, wake him and challenge him to fight by accusing him of—?' Wulfhere looked at Aidan.

'Of cheating us!' Aidan finished for him. 'I paid good money for the slaves we freed, and they are not worth what I paid!'

Wulfhere thought it sounded a bit flimsy, because the sale and purchase had been forced on Cyneard. Then he gave a wolfish grin. Details like this did not really matter, because Cyneard would be in a rage about his home being entered without consent, and it was highly unlikely he would wish to debate the issue like big brother Peada.

'He will challenge me, and—!'

'I will state it must be in the hall, where everyone can witness!' Aidan finished for him. 'Splendid!' and Wulfhere almost purred with satisfaction.

Egwina realised they had forgotten her, and she was intrigued. Who exactly was this Hoel? Why was he here? She knew that young men were often sent away to put a finish on their martial training, but which was the true young man? She had no doubt at all that he was noble. Her instinct told her this. She had admired his fine features and bold manner with his clear, vivid eyes. Something stirred in her, hidden during her troubles. In her past life, she too had had a follower. Young Cuthbert, elder son at their neighbours, had taken a fancy to her, which she had reciprocated warmly. Then her whole world had collapsed. She had often wondered what had happened to Cuthbert. He was probably dead, killed in battle—and the waste of it all. She thought of the secret she held in her heart and wondered what these two brothers would think of her if they knew. Both were the unknown quantity, and she resolved to keep her personal matters secret still, at least until she and her father were together again. Then he could advise her. First of all, though, Cyneard had to be neutralised. Was it really possible that just two men could manage this? Doubt flew through her, but she had learned to keep much to herself; not just to save her sanity but to preserve the life of herself and her beloved father.

'When?' Wulfhere rasped.

Aidan grinned at him. 'When you beat me in a sword fight, and a dagger fight and run me into the ground! It's entirely up to you!' and he looked over at Egwina. 'You have waited so long, another couple of weeks will be neither here nor there.'

That was where they were wrong, she thought with rising panic. Her father was not a strong man, and she dreaded how he had been treated, yet she was in no position to urge speed. She bowed her head and bit her lip, and accepted she had to be a little more patient.

Aidan was not quite as insensitive as Egwina thought. 'Try not to fret,' he told her kindly, 'but there are only two of us. We must be perfect, and my brother here wants just a little more practice before I let him loose against Cyneard!'

They watched her retreating back and Aidan went into deep thought. He was not quite as confident as he showed openly.

Wulfhere's mind moved in another direction: 'I can wear the sword,' he said proudly.

'Oh no you can't!'

'Why not?'

Aidan explained. 'You may be a king's son at home, but you are my brother here, just another churl and churls don't wear swords without specific permission, do they?'

Wulfhere's face fell and he flashed his companion a rueful look, then nodded. Aidan was very pleased. No sulks or scowls, just a mature decision.

'I shall carry the sword, then at the appropriate moment, toss it to you! Now the wergild!'

Wulfhere was startled. He had forgotten this valid point. He looked anxiously at Aidan.

'We agree that we are going to be provocative, to make Cyneard attack you. Initially, I just want you to defend, and I guarantee he'll then try to kill you which means you can open up. That way, there will be no Wergild to pay to the widow. It's very bad luck on her part, but I have a suspicion she will be glad to be made into a widow. Then there is compurgation to consider, isn't there?'

Wulfhere became uneasy. Legal matters could still be complicated to him, despite his past studies. Compurgation was the legal method in which an accused could be proved innocent or guilty by twelve men who swore on their treasured oaths. If found guilty, a man or his relatives would be forced to pay a heavy blood fine or even be outlawed. Once an outlaw anyone, man, woman or child, could kill with impunity. Who could compurgate for Wulfhere? Only Aidan and Egwina.

Aidan decided he had worked that one out. 'Your insult to Cyneard must be such that he antagonises you before witnesses. Leave that bit to me. Luckily this is a very small community.'

'It's all getting complicated!' Wulfhere grumbled.

'That is life!' Aidan told him unsympathetically.

CHAPTER NINE

Burhred's scowl started to deepen into a glower and his jaw set hard as Oswald continued relating everything. His eyes turned into hard chips, and even Oswald could not help but flinch. He wondered when he had last seen his friend so livid with barely suppressed anger.

Oswald held up one hand placatingly. 'I felt like you initially, but, upon reflection, what else could Aidan have done?'

Burhred, threw him a hard look. 'Dangled that boy hostage a little more before his father's eyes!' he rasped with a deep growl. If it was not first one thing, then it was another. So much for his careful plans and orchestrated effort at secrecy. It only needed one wandering churl to ride and visit Cyneard's house and all his effort would have been but nothing. More to the point, so would Wulfhere's fictitious death.

Yet he had faith and trust in Aidan. If the churl thought the proposed fight was vitally necessary Burhred knew he could not really object. Aidan was at the sharp end, while here, miles away, he could not really judge, but it was bad, and very bad. Obviously, if Aidan thought Wulfhere was going to lose the fight, he would have to step in and do the job for him, which could be equally disastrous. In the event, whatever confidence Wulfhere might have acquired would be swept away in a gale of self-doubt and personal recrimination.

As the older man, Cyneard should be the better fighter because Wulfhere was still only an untried boy and Burhred shook his head with worry. He racked his brains to recollect what he knew about Cyneard but this was very little. He was a man who had always kept a low profile for one reason or other. He paid his Hwicce tribute to Mercia without too many grumbles. It did cross his mind to wonder what Cyneard really thought now that Mercia was being forced to pay tribute to Northumbria. Was it at all possible that he might have made contact with Northumbrians? It was true such an absence would not go unnoticed but what about a messenger with written information? He wondered if the whole castle of his elaborate scheming was about to crumble about his ears. Matters political were both complicated and duplicitous.

'Aidan is correct. He must be removed or neutralised as expediently as possible. Do you know what he plans or when?'

Oswald shook his head. 'We left early the next morning before dawn, when I think you can rest easy. Aidan knows what he is doing. I have complete faith in him!'

Burhred snorted. 'I just hope you are right!' he said with an edge to his voice. 'I don't like

142

people messing up my plans with their own! Now about the girl. The adoption has been formally approved while you were away in writing, witnessed by one of the Northumbrian clerks.'

They lapsed into silence until a cunning grin was slid on to Burhred's face. 'That girl is going to be very useful to me,' he said thoughtfully. 'It won't be all that long before we have to think of winter and those months will be useful to us. When the days are short, and the weather is foul, with the people trapped in their homes for long periods, they will start to think, fester and slowly come to the boil. They will have recovered from the shock of our defeat. They will have had time to reflect upon the tribute they are being forced to pay Northumbria as reparation. They will not like it! It will stick in their proud Mercian throats. I want to hear the very first rumbles of complaint. By next spring, these will be aired in many quarters. I plan to send that girl out and about everywhere, including down to Aidan. It is vital I have detailed information on everything, everywhere and at all times.'

Oswald did not think this was a very good idea, but had sufficient sense not to air this view at present. Elfrida was hopelessly in love, a situation he considered was a lost cause. Wulfhere was not in the slightest bit interested in her existence. 'Going exactly where?'

Burhred threw him a sharp look. 'All over

our Mercian territory as well and the Hwicce lands, and at the same time I will be able to get personal reports on Wulfhere. Elfrida finds it easy to slip away unnoticed. You don't,' he pointed out.

Oswald, certainly agreed with this latter observation. Eanwulf's killer was still unknown, and he had reservations they would ever find him. He knew he had developed a tremendous affection for Elfrida. She warmed his heart, and he looked forward to the evenings with joy, but now he was concerned about her. This business of fancying Wulfhere had just about turned into an obsession with her. There was the lovely-looking girl Egwina, who was on the spot all the time and, in his opinion, it was no contest at all for Elfrida.

Once Egwina was released from slavery, after the contest, she would revert to her noble rank and be of an ideal status for Wulfhere but then what about the confidentiality matter? The trouble was, when two young people with natural hot blood were thrown into each other's company, anything could happen. So what would occur when next Elfrida rode down to that region? A little alarm bell rang but he kept this to himself. Burhred was well-known for being impatient with young love at the best of times. He would be irate if the subject were mentioned now.

Oswald realised he was in a quandary. How could he leave his friend? How could he freely let Elfrida go back down there again? He turned to study his fingernails, two of which he noted were broken. 'Any news of Eanwulf's killer?' he asked, desiring a change of subject.

Burhred shook his head, slightly puzzled. He had lost Oswald for a few moments. He had soared up onto a distant cloud over something not yet explained. For a few seconds he felt pique. If Oswald had a worry he should share it. But they were old friends, and if Oswald did not expand Burhred knew when not to press. 'No! And to give the king his due, he has tried to find him. I still plump for a travelling mercenary who will never be caught.'

'Perhaps time will tell us,' Oswald said thoughtfully. 'When nothing happens, when the killer is not discovered, he might get overconfident,' he said, and then turned aside. This meant Burhred could still be a target, despite the precautions taken. He felt uneasy. A killer in their tun was quite horrific, and his worry deepened.

'Where is that girl?' Burhred asked casually. He liked her more than he cared to let on and, deep down, would have liked to have adopted her. He was thankful now he had not because he was acutely aware of his danger. At least with Oswald she was safe, he hoped—out of her stupid brother's way.

Elfrida was not quite out of her stupid brother's way. She had gone on a casual walk, engrossed in tangled thoughts, none of which gave her much joy. She felt worse now that she had been to see Wulfhere, and desperately wished she had stayed behind. How full of hope and light-hearted she had been when she left with Oswald, and how low and miserable she felt now.

She strolled up to a place often used by the warriors for their weapons' practice. It was a clearing, not all that large, but from which most of the tall trees had been cleared and their wood utilised for fires.

She walked very quietly, from force of habit, since she liked to spy on the wild animals. Her boots were supple, with easy soles and her practised tread avoided all twigs. She was the most noiseless of her people.

There was only one fighter at practice and she was astonished to see it was her brother. She stood, partially hidden, and watched him do his spear work. A target had been fixed to one distant tree and three times Cynewulf threw his long hafted spear, and the head landed, not centre, but within a rough circle. Elfrida was impressed. He had improved enormously, because it was not the easiest of weapons to throw with any accuracy and force.

Alicia stood to one side and shouted encouragement, while her face beamed with pride. It crossed Elfrida's mind that Alicia's behaviour was that of a doting mother over a spoiled son. Did Cynewulf do everything she told him?

Then a new thought shot in mind and she watched her brother very carefully. All of a sudden, in a very short space of time, he had changed. He had certainly grown, and his body had thickened with more solid muscle. Incredible as it seemed when she had left he had been just a boy, but now he had a man's stature. Was her brother the killer? With those very powerful arm muscles, he would have no difficulty at all in hurling a spear from a distance into a man's back.

What was his motive though? She immediately dismissed the thought as rubbish. Cynewulf did not have it in him to creep up on someone and murder in cold blood. They had many warriors equally, and even better skilled with this difficult weapon, although it would be simple to inveigle Eanwulf to meet someone like him for a talk.

Elfrida still stood quietly, deeply troubled with these new worrisome thoughts. She could use the spear but not all that effectively. The weapon with which she excelled in fighting was her dagger, the long scramasax. Many tedious hours of practice had made her ambidextrous, a very rare accomplishment. She had taught herself, reasoning that the weapon, when used correctly in either hand, gave a supreme advantage as well as considerable self-confidence.

Alicia turned suddenly, sensing eyes upon

them so Elfrida stepped into view. When she saw who it was, Alicia pulled a face, then recomposed her expression into an artificial smile. 'Now what do you think of your brother?' she crowed.

Elfrida gave her back an equally false look. Each girl had natural hostility for the other without apparently any logical reason. It was true there had been spats between them in the past, but no thundering row. It was simply that they had nothing in common and, besides, Elfrida knew she felt somewhat sorry for Alicia. What kind of a person was she to chase a male so unreasonably and what kind of a brother was Cynewulf to allow this?

It flashed through her mind she was equally guilty regarding Wulfhere, yet, hopefully, she had not made quite such a crass fool of herself. Oswald knew as did Lord Burhred. The former was sympathetic in a quiet, cool way, while the latter could not have cared less. She hoped that she was now over her ridiculous obsession, while her alter ego argued how she would love to see him again but what about that lovely girl who was with him all the time?

'I think he's excellent,' she praised, knowing how Cynewulf would always expand at such praise.

Her brother beamed at her. He could not last remember when his difficult sister had tossed him one word of praise. He grinned back at her and included Alicia in this sudden happiness. 'We are going to be betrothed, and married as soon as we can,' he confided.

Alicia stifled a curse. When would Cynewulf learn to keep his mouth shut? It was her right to announce their plans, but with an effort she kept the smile fixed upon my face, although it did not reach her eyes.

'That's marvellous!' Elfrida enthused.

Alicia eyed her thoughtfully. How sincere was Elfrida, why should she mind? It was true she would now take over Sihtric's old home, but that could mean nothing to Elfrida, who had been adopted elsewhere. Sihtric's money had been meticulously divided by the Witan, and even the cottars and gerbers had been apportioned a sum. Elfrida was now a very good catch for some man and Alicia itched to meddle.

'Yes!' she replied tersely.

Now what was biting her, Elfrida wondered? Brother Cynewulf, you are welcome to what you are going to get but you will never be your own man, she thought to herself. How long would it take Cynewulf to become fed up with this state of affairs? And if it came down to matrimonial warfare was he strong enough to stand up against Alicia? She had a sudden sneaking suspicion that once the initial marital glow had been replaced by rows, Cynewulf would remember they were siblings and expect her to be his ally. Oh no, you don't, she told herself. He was going to make his own bed, and on it he would lie—without her.

She threw them both a nod, then turned on her heel and sauntered back the way she had come.

'She's a rude old thing. I can't stand her!' Alicia snapped.

Cynewulf had a lot more affection for his sister that anyone considered possible. She was his only true flesh and blood. 'Don't take any notice. It's just her way!' he said placatingly.

Alicia scowled at him in exasperation. Was she doing the right thing by picking him instead of one of the more dominant Northumbrians? If only Cynewulf had a bit more go and initiative: then it hit her, if he did, she would no longer be the boss.

Elfrida returned home and felt thoroughly out of sorts. What exactly was going on down in the Hwicce territory right now? How much authority did Aidan actually have over Wulfhere? She itched to go and see Burhred and ask him but didn't quite dare. If only her wonderful father had not died, life would have been so much simpler. Even with her new adopted father, there were times when she felt bitterly alone with miserable thoughts, when she simply did not know what to do next.

CHAPTER TEN

Aidan did. They all crowded into the house, which still held a pleasant smell of fresh cut timbers. Wulfhere sat on a stool. Aidan stood. Egwina placed herself against one wall, while Alcium and Edith stood close together against the other wall.

'Timing is vital!' Aidan told them, going over it all for the last time. After consultation with Wulfhere, they had taken Alcium and Edith into their plans, suspecting accurately that Egwina would already have confided in Edith, as they had become friends. 'We will be heavily outnumbered so one mistake and we might well go down!' He refrained from adding that Wulfhere's cover would also be blown, which could lead to tragic consequences. As things stood, the others had all accepted he was here teaching his younger brother Hoel everything he knew about warfare. This was logical and acceptable to them all.

'We will leave on horse, just before dawn breaks. Cyneard's sentry will not be expecting anyone and most likely will be asleep. I will stun him because it is vital he makes no call of alarm. Everyone with me?' Aidan asked and looked around to receive nods of assent.

'You, Egwina, make sure you have pieces of

meat with you. Your job is to keep the hounds quiet, so you'll have to go in the lead. Once you've done this, they won't bay or howl. Now what's next?' he asked firmly, and looked at Egwina.

She blushed and felt her heart race. 'I sneak around to where my father was always kept with the other slaves. I will have my knife. I am to wait in the shadows. As soon as anyone enters to help Cyneard, I am to give this knife to my father for action.'

Aidan nodded with satisfaction and turned his attention to Alcium. 'You!'

'I keep with you and your brother and my job is to make sure Raebald does not try any dirty, underhand trick,' he said for the fourth time. He was just about word perfect as Aidan had been drilling them for ages, but Alcium approved. It was a sound policy to make quite sure that everyone knew exactly what they had to do, where and when.

Wulfhere chipped in: 'I go to Cyneard's sleeping chamber, barge in like a bull and bellow at him for cheating us!'

Aidan was so pleased he almost purred. 'There is just one point, Cyneard's wife, daughter and the female slaves.'

Egwina spoke. 'Remember there are only two, and they are middle-aged. They will be too cowed to do anything. You see, they were born slaves and have no spirit left. I can't say I blame them after a life under Cyneard,' she added with empathy. 'It is the same with Julie and Ygraine, her daughter, poor things. They won't make any trouble. They will be too terrified,' she prophesied.

Aidan thought of the sword. He had worked out how Wulfhere was to fight, and with which weapons, drilling him mercilessly and he was confident about his young charge's ability. Deep in his heart, he was secretly delighted for this opportunity to blood Wulfhere, though, stifling a smile, he could well imagine Burhred's fury.

'Very well,' he ended. 'Just all get a few hours' sleep, have a very light meal and, Alcium, you get the horses ready. Then we go!'

Once they were alone again Aidan turned to Wulfhere, very serious now. 'You are in my sole charge. I have complete authority over you,' he began.

Wulfhere nodded, suddenly feeling uneasy. What was Aidan going to come out with? And the latent, dull suspicion flared. 'Cyneard is mine and mine alone!' he said sharply.

Aidan stared back and said nothing for a moment. His eyes were steady. 'Just you make sure you win, as I have planned, otherwise—' and he let the end of the sentence hang in the air. 'And wipe that stubborn look off your face or I'll do it for you with this!' he rasped, showing one great hand balled into an even larger fist.

Wulfhere backed down momentarily and

153

flashed a wry smile, because he understood. Aidan could not afford to let him die yet for the sake of Mercia and, personally, he wanted to win on his own merit—as a king in waiting. It would be the forerunner of many battles to come. He knew in his bones that the whole of his future life could revolve around what took place in the next handful of hours. He felt confident. Who would not after receiving Aidan's extremely harsh training? He was harder and tougher with powerful muscles, which had grown with the exercises. His lungs had stretched with all the running, and he knew he was taller and weighed more. He was a man now.

* * *

They left as pre-planned in pitch dark with only the suggestion of dawn in the east. Their approach was unhurried and silent. When within sight of the house, they dismounted, hobbled their animals and padded forward as a long crocodile, with Egwina in the lead.

As Aidan had already guessed it had been another long, boring night for the sentry. He leaned against the outside fence in a very light sleep. Aidan stole up and slugged him with his fist, then caught his unconscious body, lowering it softly to the earth.

Egwina stepped up, carrying a bag that held plenty of raw meat. She opened it out and wafted the meat's scent in the air as Aidan unfastened the gate silently. Four hounds came running, hackles erect, jaws open to display wicked teeth, then they caught Egwina's scent. Their sterns wagged enthusiastically, and one went to bark a greeting. Swiftly, Egwina tossed the meat as far from her as she could, and the hounds bounded after it. The animals, like the slaves, were also half-starved.

The invaders walked forward more confidently. As Egwina had known, the door was not locked, so they crowded quietly through it while Egwina, knife in hand, slid around to the slave quarters. Edith carefully positioned herself in the shadows, from where she could watch and warn. Aidan nodded approvingly, and they stepped into a fairly large, but very gloomy hall.

At the far end some embers still glowed red and Alcium tiptoed forward, lit two candles and placed them in the night sockets fixed on the wall. He held his spear at the ready, and Aidan nodded to Wulfhere.

Wulfhere sprang forward with thudding heart and rising excitement. He slammed open the cubicle door and let out a roar. 'Cheat.'

Cyneard received the biggest shock of his life. He awoke violently, and it took him a few seconds to collect scattered wits, then he scrambled to his feet, hardly able to believe his eyes. 'What the hell do you think you're doing in my home?' he bellowed back.

'Foul cheat!' Wulfhere threw at him, adding a few oaths for good measure. 'You took our money and that female is no good at all. You tried to make out you didn't want to sell, but all the time you just wanted to offload her!'

Cyneard recovered very quickly. What exactly this was all about he was not quite clear but he was livid. His natural, vile temper exploded. He jumped forward and smashed Wulfhere across one cheek, and both retreated into the little hall, where he used his fist again.

Aidan stepped forward. 'I saw that!' he said smoothly. This was better than he had hoped. 'My brother has no arms in his hands. You struck him for nothing instead of debating a matter when he made a legitimate complaint. And don't challenge us coming in like this. If we had come in broad daylight you would have made yourself scarce, wouldn't you?' he jeered.

'Raebald!' Cyneard shouted. 'Get the slaves and arm them!'

There was a flurry of activity from another side cubicle, where the equally startled Raebald also awoke violently. He came outside hastily pulling on his trousers, half-hopping on one foot.

'I never said the girl was good. That's your own fault for being too quick!' Cyneard growled.

'You were quick enough to take a generous

payment, you cheating thief!' Wulfhere hurled back at him. 'We'll have our money returned!'

Cyneard went scarlet with anger as Raebald returned with some sleepy-eyed slaves who held small spears as if they were toys. At their rear was a very tall, haggard man, confused, but with eyes that brightened suddenly. A woman appeared with a frightened girl. 'Get back!' Cyneard roared and, trembling, they did.

'Now stay, everyone!' Aidan shouted. 'Stay and be a witness, all of you. Me and my brother have been cheated. There is also the matter of fact that you ordered that girl there to poison us. Or, if that failed, to use a sword on us. You have planned murder more than once!' Wulfhere pointed to the sword where it hung loosely from Aidan's belt.

Cyneard was badly jolted now, speechless for a few seconds, while his mind raced. They were in the wrong bursting in like this, but as they had made the girl talk they had wrong-footed him completely. Who would a Court of Compurgators believe? He had a sudden sick feeling it would not be him because he was known to be harsh and cruel. He was so frustrated at paying non-stop tribute to Mercia, his only pleasure came from operating his little fiefdom with malice. He knew he enjoyed inflicting pain, as did Raebald; it was just a hobby to them. He suspected that twelve good men and true would neither believe him, nor agree with his type of life. He hesitated uncertainly, then his temper flared again.

'You wet behind the ears puppy!' he snarled at Wulfhere. 'You want some manners teaching you and I'm just the right man to do it. You'll fight?' he challenged hopefully.

Wulfhere pretended to hesitate as Aidan had instructed and in a mild tone gave a nod. 'Yes!'

'What weapons?' Cyneard growled, running his eyes over the body facing him. A young, fit body, but Cyneard's confidence grew. A youngster who knew nothing, but thought he knew it all.

Wulfhere pretended to consider. 'Axe and knife!' he suggested quietly.

Now Aidan took a hand in the proceedings. 'This hall will do, before everyone as witnesses!' and he half-turned to Raebald, who held a spear menacingly now. 'And you can go over there, and stand next to one of my men,' he said forcefully.

Cyneard did not miss the play on words. Just how many of them lurked outside? He cursed violently. That fool girl should have acted more quickly and he wanted to get his hands on her. Then he saw her standing with her stubborn father. 'Get over here!' he roared.

'Stay exactly where you are!' Aidan bellowed. 'I give the orders to her right now. Not you!' and he glowered at Cyneard.

Aidan felt a fresh wave of worry. Despite how Wulfhere had grown, he was inclined to look very insignificant against such a powerful, mature male. Aidan quietly withdrew the sword. It balanced well in the hand, and he saw the tall, haggard man's eyes open wide at sight of it.

'To the death?' Cyneard challenged.

Wulfhere nodded with forced casualness. Now the time had come he itched to start, but he made himself remember all of Aidan's advice.

Aidan turned on the onlookers. 'You all heard!' he said sternly. 'You might have to give evidence about this one day in a court!' he warned strongly.

Cyneard backed to a wall on which hung a variety of weapons, mostly for decoration, but all still lethal and genuine. He selected an axe and a knife, and Aidan passed his own weapons to Wulfhere but kept the sword in his right hand, making it very obvious he would not hesitate to use it if necessary.

More natural light had now filtered in through the window slits. The woman and her child had re-appeared and huddled together to one side, where they could also watch. Aidan wondered at their thoughts. The more witnesses the better, in his opinion. He eyed the slaves sternly, but saw that Egwina's father had understood the situation exactly. He had pushed his daughter behind him and stood with her knife held easily balanced, either for undercutting or for a quick reversal to be thrown. Their eyes met for a second and Aidan gave him a quick nod of approval.

Cyneard studied the opposition more closely now. Somehow this had all escalated to more than he intended, yet he knew he was the wronged one—except for the orders he had given the girl. It was all her fault, and his anger boiled, while his eyes bored into those of Wulfhere. Here was youth, fitness, fast reflexes and training, but, he guessed, little actual experience. Cyneard knew every dirty trick in the book, and he had no hesitation at all in playing them—as long as he won.

Wulfhere examined him in turn. He certainly was a powerful man, but even then he could not match Aidan. He flexed his muscles, took some deep breaths to steady himself and tried to remember all of his trainer's advice. He was not nervous, if anything he was keen to start, but Aidan had disciplined him well.

Egwina was frankly terrified out of her wits. If the young man and then his brother were beaten she knew her life was forfeit to Cyneard, and her father would be helpless. So much depended upon the next few minutes, and her heart hammered in terror. Her father with but a knife would be able to do little. He might take one man out, but the others would not hesitate to overpower him; their whole welfare was at stake. Cyneard had a very long and exceedingly ugly memory.

Aidan threw one more look around, hunting for treachery, then studied the combatants. He was pleased with Wulfhere's stance, but he could see a nerve throbbing in his neck. Apprehension or keenness? Cyneard seemed cool enough, but his cheeks were far too red, while his eyes burned with rage.

Everyone else huddled against the walls. Julie held her daughter in her arms, shielding the child's eyes from what was to come.

'Start!' Aidan cried and Cyneard leaped forward, axe in his right hand, knife in his left. Wulfhere let him come, bracing himself with one foot slightly behind the other, his own axe raised. The two weapons met with a crash; each haft throbbing against the other while both men tried a low knife attack against the guts.

Foiled, they half circled and broke free. Wulfhere sprang forward, eyes highly alert and for a second time the weapons collided. Cyneard pressed down hard, his muscles pushing Wulfhere's weapon lower, then he half-stepped forward to bring himself within knife range. Wulfhere neatly side-stepped and swung with his lower left hand. His knife blade scored along Cyneard's right forearm, opening the skin in a long wound. It was minor, but the first blood.

Cyneard winced slightly and changed tactics. He swung with his axe, but it was a fake blow. Wulfhere stepped forward, in anticipation to duck under the blow when Cyneard closed unexpectedly, body to body. The older, more cunning man hooked a foot around one ankle, then gave a mighty shove with his body weight. Wulfhere went toppling backwards, his axe leaving his hand.

Wulfhere had one heartbeat now to save his life as Cyneard swung his axe downwards in a lethal blow. Wulfhere rolled frantically aside and shot to his feet with youth's agility but his feet slipped a little on the old rushes. With a bellow of triumph, Cyneard swung and charged forward, hitting downwards. Raebald saw the opportunity, with everyone distracted in horror. Before it was possible to intercept, he withdrew his knife and skilfully threw it. As Wulfhere scrabbled to keep his feet, the knife plunged into the fleshy part of his left arm. He halted instinctively, and Cyneard struck again, positive of victory.

Aidan withdrew the sword and charged forward, but knew he could not be in time. In the next two heartbeats Wulfhere had to die. Alcium moved and stabbed his spear into Raebald's side as general fighting broke out. Egwina's father used the knife frantically. Egwina kicked with both feet, bit and scratched, then Wulfhere had jumped out of range, recovered from the knife wound's shock, and faced Cyneard's optimistic charge forward.

He ducked under the descending axe and brought his knee up savagely into Cyneard's testicles. The older man braked abruptly, screamed and doubled in agony. Wulfhere's knife travelled forward and up. It was a blow travelling fast and hard and it ruptured the great artery, the aorta, as it continued upwards.

Cyneard knew he was dying on his feet. Aidan skidded to a halt, saw what was going on behind and charged forward to where Alcium and Egwina's father stood fighting desperately, shoulder to shoulder. Then Aidan was among the slaves, roaring his anger, the flat of his sword blade smashing against heads. Wulfhere stood while blood poured from the arm wound and, suddenly, terrified afresh, the slaves capitulated and dropped to their knees in submission.

Cyneard's body lay on the trampled rushes, bled dry. Wulfhere streamed with his own blood from the fresh wound. Alcium had a facial swelling, which would deliver a huge black eye in the morning while Egwina's father was quite unscathed, except he breathed hard and sweat dappled his forehead.

Aidan whipped around in a tight circle, eyes darting everywhere but it was all over. Egwina stood alongside her father, panting heavily while Alcium grunted with pleasure. It had been good to fight again, as a man of Mercia and not a slave.

Raebald lay untidily dead at Alcium's feet. Aidan took a deep breath, strode over, threw a cursory glance at Wulfhere's wound and sniffed. It was nothing.

'That was a close-run thing,' he observed to no one in particular, 'and you still have some learning to do!'

Wulfhere felt acutely embarrassed. He was honest enough to realise he had been very near to death, through his own carelessness. He should have anticipated Cyneard's dirty tricks. 'I made a bit of a muck of it all,' he admitted ruefully, 'but I'll get better. No one will pull a stunt like that on me ever again!' he vowed.

Aidan knew self-recrimination was more beneficial than anything he could say. He slapped his companion on his good shoulder. 'You should just have seen the balls-up I made of my first fight!' he confided with a grin. 'Now let's get that flesh wound dressed against infection.'

Egwina came over, her hand in that of her father. He stood before them, and bowed his head to the victorious brothers. 'I presume I belong to you both?' he asked, addressing them in turn.

Wulfhere flashed a look at Aidan, then grinned back. 'No you don't!' he said gently. 'You belong to your daughter. How are you called though?'

The skeletally thin man smiled gently back.

164

'Ceol!' he replied to Wulfhere who stood while Aidan washed the arm wound from a small container of water, which Alcium had produced and into which Edith had sprinkled some dried herbs, providentially carried in anticipation of their need.

Aidan kept one beady eye on the slaves. They stayed on their knees, trembling at the thought of their new fate. Julie and her daughter shivered together, eyes averted from the two corpses.

'Alcium, get those slaves to take the bodies out of here, and then I want the slaves back. Edith, go and keep an eye on this place from the outside, will you, just in case anyone rides up?'

Shortly all were in the little hall again except Edith. A tight bandage had staunched Wulfhere's bleeding, and, together, the brothers faced everyone.

Egwina's relief was almost palpable. For Ceol, it was all still rather hard to take in. Everything had happened too unexpectedly and too quickly. He was still in a state of shock and stood in a rather bemused state of disbelief. Everyone there knew the rule of "Winner takes all".

Wulfhere needed no prompting on what to do next. He followed his instincts and let his eyes drift over the frightened group of slaves. 'Was this a fair fight?'

Heads nodded in unison, so Wulfhere

continued. 'Will you all swear to that at the next sitting of the Hundred Court, if it should be necessary?' he demanded coldly.

The slaves looked at each other, as did Egwina and Ceol. There was an uneasy silence, and the slaves looked anxiously at each other. Who dared to speak out? One man snatched at what little courage slavery had left him.

'Sirs, we will all swear to that. But we cannot give our oaths, because as slaves, we have none to give!' he blurted out with fear.

Wulfhere looked at the man, and remembered when his father had sometimes addressed a gathering, using the magnetic power of his personality. He copied. His eyes travelled from one to the other, slowly but forcefully. No one could hold his gaze. When he considered they were sufficiently cowed he altered his mien.

'I am the victor! You all belong to me by my right of battle success!' This was not something he had rehearsed with Aidan. It flashed across his mind to wonder why, then guessed his close companion had decided to leave him to play his own part. It was a test. That was fine by him and his confidence soared.

'I free you all,' Wulfhere pronounced in a solemn and loud voice. Every bowed head shot up, and he was stared at with huge, amazed and hopeful eyes . . . 'On one condition!'

Wulfhere paused solemnly, instinctively, building up a dramatic atmosphere. They all held their breaths and wondered what was coming next. 'As you are now all free men, you have an oath to give. If you all voluntarily swear your oaths of loyalty and fealty to me, here and now, your lives will be totally different!'

Aidan was delighted. This was a classic example of breeding showing, but he said nothing and continued to scrutinise everyone for possible treachery.

'I will gladly swear!' cried the man who had first spoken. 'Me too!' echoed a second and the slaves all stepped forward in a ragged line. They remembered long-forgotten manners and bowed their heads to the brothers, raised their right hands, and swore to serve faithfully and loyally.

Wulfhere returned just a tiny head bow of acknowledgement, then smiled warmly. He was pleased with himself and a quick look at Aidan showed he was also delighted. He was not so naive that he failed to realise these men must still be watched until they had proved their merit, but it was a start.

Then he turned to Cyneard's wife and daughter. He walked over, avoiding the red-stained rushes, and read stark fear, and shook his head. 'Don't worry, madam. No harm will come to you here at all and certainly no rape. However, I must point out that it was your husband challenged me and it was his specific wish to fight to the death so there will be no wergild payment due.' He paused and watched her. 'Raebald heard this, but he is also dead. I have no proof that what I say is the truth, but I do affirm it,' he ended, and waited.

Julie was lost for words. Surely this was all a ghastly nightmare from which she would awaken at any minute to discover Cyneard was still around. Her marriage, which had started off so hopefully on her part, had turned into a horrific fiasco from the very start. It was only when she had entered his house that she been able to see Cyneard for the ogre he was. A violent, evil man, with more natural cruelty in his make-up than she thought any one person could possibly have. Now he was gone. She was free from him for ever! The lack of wergild meant nothing when tallied against this new lease of life.

'What is going to happen to us?' she asked in a nervous voice.

Wulfhere and Aidan had both seen fear before but never such raw terror as was reflected in another human being's eyes. Wulfhere gave her a gentle smile and spoke softly.

'This is your home and here you will stay. We will get your son back as quickly as possible,' he told her but began to pick his words with care, acutely aware of his own position. 'My brother and myself will arrange

168

this.' He turned and threw a questioning look at Ceol, beckoning him to come forward and join them. 'Perhaps Ceol can move into your house, as well as his daughter. If you don't have the spare chambers, then we can arrange to have two built,' he suggested smoothly.

Julie realised she was being given a delicate, highly tactful order, but she did not mind. She had often felt for this man as well as the other slaves. If this victor and his brother meant what they said, and she was inclined to believe both of them, their lives could only change for the better.

Wulfhere turned to Ceol. 'From where do you come?'

Ceol gave a heavy sigh. 'Another lifetime ago, I had my own manor in the southeast,' he explained sadly. 'I will be happy to stay here, though, with my daughter,' he reassured, and looked kindly at Julie. 'I think we have both had more than our fair share of suffering,' he mused aloud. 'Perhaps it is time to bring a new atmosphere to this house?'

Julie looked hopefully at him. She could tell from the way he spoke he was both educated and cultured. Cyneard had been crude, almost like one of his own pigs, yet he had been able to flatter her father into getting her hand in matrimony. She vowed she would never think about it again. This was a chance for a new beginning. She nodded as her heart lifted.

Wulfhere took a deep breath, turned his

back on them, and marched over to Aidan. He was conscious of some pain in his arm, but his expression was bland. He stood before his companion, and his eyes asked a silent question.

Aidan gave him a grin of pleasure and slapped his back. 'Very good indeed!' he hissed in a low voice. 'Your respected father could not have done better, and I don't think even grumpy Burhred would be able to carp too much!' he praised lavishly.

Later, when his pupil's wound had healed, he intended to give him physical hell and spend considerable time teaching him every dirty trick known to man, and how to counteract them. Right now, though, this had all gone off far better than he had ever dared to hope. Burhred must be told and that they would discuss later.

'We will leave you then,' Aidan said meaningfully and flashed a look at Ceol that asked him to take complete control in their absence. Then another went to Alcium, and they walked outside, where Edith joined them.

It was broad daylight, with the sun shining, but the air still had a slight edge to it. It was obvious that winter was going to come early. Aidan did not mind. Indeed, he hoped the snow would be thick. They would all be completely isolated down here, cut off from all men, but that made it essential to get word to Burhred quickly.

170

When the brothers were alone again Aidan explained what he had in mind and Wulfhere listened carefully. He thought for a moment, then made his own comment. 'I think he can be trusted,' he said slowly, hoping he was correct.

Aidan nodded grimly. 'It's not too much of a risk, because we'll have something that outsells another hostage, won't we?' he chuckled. 'Lord Burhred must be all stewed up wondering what has happened here. So it's vital he is told. I would also like to know if the murderer has been found.'

Wulfhere wanted to know that as well. As they walked back to their hut it seemed strange to realise they were at last by themselves, which was what they wanted in the first place. Egwina would stay with her father but he guessed they would not be short of good, hot food. His heart warmed at the thought of Egwina. On the days when Aidan had not worked him too hard, he had yearned for female company of his own age. Now that she was free, and under her father's wing again, he had every excuse to ride and see her. He realised his thoughts were now moving onto a romantic plain, and he began to do a bit of daydreaming.

'Alcium!' Aidan bawled lustily, standing by their door. 'Over here!'

Alcium bounded over and the brothers reflected on his change. He was bright-eyed, fresh-faced and shaved every morning with his knife. He stood tall and proud, as a man assured. There was more flesh on his frame from the good food, and he was highly alert at all times.

The three of them went inside, sat while Aidan poured them all some ale. Edith had brewed it and it was still a little raw, but it made a refreshing drink.

'You say you are a Mercian!' Aidan began carefully. 'From which part of our lands though?'

Alcium was a little puzzled but he had learned that Aidan did not waste his breath on futile questions. He always had a reason.

'From the far north of our lands,' he explained, 'and I've been gone for so many years, and I doubt anyone would recognise me,' he said carefully.

Aidan threw him a sharp look. 'Does that matter?' he drawled alertly.

Alcium tossed him a grin. 'I think you want me to do something and go somewhere?' he guessed. 'I will be pleased to help in every way. Without you two brothers—' and he shook his head. 'I think we would both have been dead from starvation or disease in another year,' he said soberly. 'You have given us back our lives and our debt to both of you is heavy.'

Aidan nodded. 'That boy hostage is to be released and brought back to his mother. I'll tell you exactly where to go and give you an authority in writing to explain the circumstances so you don't get speared for abduction!' He grinned. 'But before that I have a long, rather complicated return message to go to someone else, with no questions asked!' and now his voice held a warning.

Alcium scented the mystery was getting deep. He nodded and waited. Aidan took his time, and eyed him steadily, but he was as sure of this man as anyone could be. He had given his oath, any man's most treasured possession before that of wife, son, sword or best horse.

Edith could stay with them. They could soon put up a rough partition and Edith would have to be hostage for her man's return and their safety.

Aidan knew Alcium was sharp enough to understand and to accept what was, after all, perfectly normal behaviour. 'Edith will stay here with us. By nightfall, there will be a private partition for her and she will be under our joint guardianship.'

Alcium understood completely without any resentment. Who exactly these brothers were he had not the faintest idea, and decided he did not really want to know. They obviously had very good reasons for wishing to be secretive and alone, which he found perfectly acceptable. Edith would be kept here hostage for him. Any treachery on his part, and there would be no hesitation about the brothers killing her. These were two very hard men especially the senior. Only a fool would choose their enmity instead of their friendship and Alcium was nobody's fool.

CHAPTER ELEVEN

Elfrida eyed Burhred. He seemed to be upset, and she guessed it was a health matter. After they had broken their fast in their comfortable threesome, she had watched him limp heavily to his favourite seat. He seemed so very old to her, and she guessed the joint ills were striking him heavily. Already, she wondered about the winter to come. In the mornings, although still only autumn, there was a distinct cold nip of frost, which was very early.

She looked around the house, now her home too, with her own cubicle for sleeping and dressing. It was as well insulated as anyone knew how to make a home in those days but, when the days were short and the freezing nights on them, they would all have to sleep dressed. Very little washing was done then, and after a few weeks Elfrida knew she would smell but that didn't matter, because they were all the same. At least, in such cold, the lice and fleas did not thrive either. She remembered stories of ancient times, when the Romans had lived in the island, and how comfortable their homes had been. They'd even had hot water and heated floors and took baths regularly. Sometimes when it was particularly miserable she wished men knew how to construct the civilised Roman amenities but the skills had been lost when the Romans left after their 400 years of occupation.

If heavy rain came first, before it turned very cold, the cruel frosts and blizzards were guaranteed to follow. It was a time when the walls of their homes dripped water from the condensation caused by the cooking fire. Mould would grow on clothing, and anything not used daily. This became a time when only the most important work kept men outside. The cattle as well as their other precious domestic animals had to be guarded against the wolves. Inside their homes, people would huddle up near the fire and each other, making this or that, under rush lights or candles, and it was a time when tempers rose and quarrels broke out. A long, bitter winter usually also meant the mouth illness struck— the one in which the teeth could loosen or their gums become red and swollen.

Their diet would be meat with whatever grain they had been able to preserve and stop from getting the poisonous green mould. Without fresh green foods their mouths and teeth suffered, but it was simply one of the hazards of a diet composed of salted or smoked meat with a little grain gruel and

175

whatever unleaven bread they could make. She hated the winter, like everyone else, and like them she had to endure.

Her mind turned to Cynewulf. He really wanted to marry before the winter set in, and her feelings were mixed. She felt so sorry for him, because deep down was Alicia the right person? There were times when she allowed herself the indulgence of a good wallow in self-pity. Sometimes she thought she would never marry. Certainly, no matter how hard she looked around the tun there was not one young man who took her fancy. No male had ever stirred her emotions as had Wulfhere of Mercia.

There were times when she sank into the pit of despondency, and only Oswald really understood. He never said a word as there was nothing practical for him to say. And she knew he had not mentioned anything of this to Burhred because, like herself, he was concerned at the elder's downward slide into poor health. There were times when Oswald nearly went into a panic, afraid that Burhred might not live long enough to see Wulfhere return. That would be cruel irony and leave just him, Ealstan and Elfrida as trusted allies of the young pretender. When Wulfhere could be summoned back he must return at the most propitious time and, in Oswald's eyes, that might not be too easy to judge. It certainly would not be this year at all. As he walked around the tun he sensed the Mercian defeat still lay like a smothering cloth over the people. They paid their tribute to Northumbria, and did not yet grumble. Let this just go on though, Oswald told himself, especially after a bad winter, and matters might reflect a lot more differently on the people's emotions.

There were no Northumbrians here now, for which everyone was thankful. King Oswiu was nobody's fool. He was astute enough not to lean too hard on defeated peoples, knowing that snap visits were far more unsettling and demoralising than leaving soldiers or clerks in a place permanently. With the advent of the bad weather, and knowing how much worse it would be in more northerly Northumbria, Oswald calculated they would not see their overmasters again until spring.

So on this particular morning, they sat in relative peace with each other when a servant, a newly freed slave, came and spoke to Burhred. He advised him there was a strange man, just ridden in, who wished to have speech with him.

Now what, Burhred asked himself? Someone trying to arrange some last-minute autumn trading? He did not want anything, but agreed to see the stranger, waving to Oswald and Elfrida to stay.

The man who entered was a total stranger because Burhred had an excellent memory for faces. The stranger eyed the others who were there, then spoke firmly to the senior man. 'I was ordered to speak to you only,' he said respectfully.

Burhred eyed him. This was a clean, strong type of man, probably a churl, who made the backbone of Mercia. 'Who sent you?'

Alcium said just one word, which galvanised all three of them into high alertness. 'Aidan!' and he reached in the secret pocket of the inside of his tunic to hand over a small scroll.

Burhred eyed it with suspicion, carefully examined the seal, then opened it. He pulled a face and started to read very slowly because clever Aidan had used the simple code he had devised. There was not a sound, as he read, but once finished Burhred sat back and stared hard at Alcium.

'So!' Burhred began. 'You are a Mercian who had to sell himself into slavery, but have now been freed. This—' and he waved the scroll '—says you are loyal to me if I wish this?'

Alcium was a little disturbed. What exactly he had expected to find when he arrived had worried him a little. This elder's hard stare disconcerted him. From the old man emanated a wave of total ruthlessness, and he felt a flicker of alarm. He was also conscious of the other man's eyes fixed on him with a peculiar expression. Hadn't he seen them both before? He went back in his mind, and now recognised them from the previous visit. What exactly was going on here? 'Loyal to you and Mercia!' he stated.

Burhred did not mince his words. 'I hope so otherwise you won't live long,' he said coldly. 'What exactly do you know?'

Alcium swallowed nervously and waggled his shoulders a little. 'Nothing, sir!' he hastened to say. Quite suddenly, he felt in the greatest danger without knowing exactly why. 'There are two men, brothers, who came and settled in the area. From what I have gathered I believe you know the rest,' he said, and nodded at the scroll.

Burhred did indeed. Initially, he had been furious at the man's arrival until his commonsense told him Aidan had to know what he was doing, because he was the man on the spot. The trouble was, Burhred admitted to himself, his naturally suspicious nature had grown since Eanwulf's murder. He was inclined to question all men and their activities, as well as look for double meanings in verbal statements. He hesitated just a moment longer, then made up his mind.

'There is a lot happening about which you will not know, because of your slavery,' he began carefully. 'Some of us do not like this and are planning certain steps to rectify and change a bad situation from getting worse— for the sake of our race and our tribe. We are not yet slaves to Northumbria, despite having to pay heavy tribute but are rapidly heading that way, unless particular plans come to fruition, which cannot be yet awhile for a multiplicity of reasons. Because of this, while you are here, you do not mention by word or deed from where you come, or that two brothers have taken up residence there,' he said harshly. 'Lives depend upon your still tongue!' and now his voice became almost savage with emotion.

Alcium was completely bewildered, and even felt his personal danger increase. Then his natural honesty flared and he returned the elder's cold gaze with one of his own. 'First of all, sir, I do not talk, never have. That is the first thing a badly treated slave learns for his own survival. Then, he also goes very deaf indeed—if he has any sense—but, most important of all, when freedom does come again he gives his oath to serve. Behind that oath is his own life, given voluntarily,' he said with considerable dignity.

Burhred eyed him, then something shone in his eyes, and he relaxed and nodded approval. 'Well spoken!' he praised. 'I have complete faith in Aidan's judgment, so I believe you. Your tight lips now become responsible for many people living decent, natural lives.' Then he turned to Elfrida. 'You will have met before? And you are going to see a lot more of her in the future. She is my trusted courier!'

Elfrida blinked. This was news to her, and not particularly palatable. She threw a

180

questioning look at Burhred who chose to ignore it, so something cold slid down her spine.

Burhred concentrated upon Alcium. 'It is vital I have a good liaison link, and this girl can slip in and out of anywhere without a person being the wiser. She will also ride circuit for me on a regular basis when the weather is fit.'

Elfrida's heart sank lower. How could she? Why should she? Every time she saw Wulfhere her heart was going to be torn, yet how could she not obey a direct order? What made this worse was the fact that there really was no one else. Oswald would not leave his friend now, and Ealstan was probably a little bit too old for such a job with all the riding involved.

Alcium glanced at the girl, who studied the toes of her boots. She did not look at all enthusiastic and, anyhow, what was a girl doing involved in what looked like a very complicated game of some kind or another? His mystification deepened, but he knew he dared not probe. He always had Edith to consider, held hostage for him even if it had been done very politely.

Burhred understood his general bewilderment. 'All will become clear to you in due course, but I do not want you here longer than necessary. You may stay overnight in the guesthouse and eat with us, then you must go back quickly. If anyone should question you, you are but a wandering churl. Be casual, even offhand.'

Alcium nodded. That was reasonable because churls did wander, as was their right. 'When I leave in the morning. I have to go by the circuitous route, because I have to collect the abducted boy and return him to his mother. You lady will be back before me,' and he looked at Elfrida.

Burhred nodded. A word from Aidan would seal the mother's lips. But he still felt very uneasy. What had started out as a secret between but a handful of people appeared to have escalated far and wide. He was realistic enough to know he could do nothing about this, just chance to luck.

'Elfrida, show him the guest house,' he snapped peremptorily. All of a sudden, he wanted this man outside, suitably hidden, so he could have Oswald to himself. When the two of them were alone he brought his friend up-to-date. Oswald considered the news and shook his head.

'It's all very unfortunate but it can't be helped. At least, with the bad weather coming, there will be nobody travelling around, so hopefully it can all remain secret. At least until spring. There's something else I don't like,' Oswald told him. 'It's Elfrida, she is head over heels in love with Wulfhere, who doesn't even know she exists. Especially now there's a lovely girl of noble status, who is going to be available to him every day!'

Burhred grunted. 'I worked that one out myself quite a while ago, but I am afraid I don't give a damn about Elfrida's feelings. I have some too, you know!' and he nodded at his swollen knee joints. 'Ill-health feelings, but they won't stop me from working the plan to fulfilment. If Elfrida is silly enough to become heart-sick over someone she can't catch, then that is tough. She will have to learn to live with it and look elsewhere. No girl's emotions will thwart me. I have worked too long and too hard for all this. Before I die I want to see Wulfhere as Mercia's legitimate king, and our people free from the yoke of Northumbria.'

Oswald knew there was nothing more to say. It was a reaction he had expected, but with his wonderful daughter's best interests at heart, he felt unhappy for her.

Burhred read his mind then. 'And don't you go taking your new father's duties too seriously either. The girl will get over her heartache. It won't kill her. Peada might!' he rasped unsympathetically. 'Find me something on which to write. I have to send a message back to Aidan. The girl can carry it if that man is going to get the hostage boy.'

Elfrida felt depressed and, as always, sought solitude. She set out for a brisk walk and immediately bumped into her brother.

'Just the person I wanted to see,' Cynewulf began, his face brightening as he fell into step with her. 'Do me a favour!' he pleaded.

Elfrida halted, turned and faced him warily. 'Such as?'

Cynewulf fumbled for words, temporarily embarrassed, then they came out in a rush. 'I want some money,' he said, and knew his cheeks flamed.

Elfrida was astounded. 'What on earth for?'

Cynewulf gave a little shrug. 'Well, you see, I think Alicia is so wonderful and I want my Morning Gift to be the best ever but that will leave me short of money. Can you let me have a loan?'

Elfrida was stunned. 'From where?' she asked sarcastically.

Cynewulf had already worked that out. 'Split your gerber rents with me for half a year, will you? You don't need money, with your new adoptive father. Anyhow, you already have your half share of everything our father owned and you're not getting married!'

Elfrida could hardly believe what she was hearing. She opened her mouth to give him a violent refusal, then saw the silent pleading in his eyes. It hit her as a huge blow. Dear Spirits, she told herself, he is afraid of Alicia! She was horrified and her heart went out to him. So often in the past, when he had been young, it had been she who would dry his eyes, and croon a story to him. Even when they quarrelled she had always known she could not be really harsh with him. So now it stuck in her throat that someone she disliked had her brother in a state of fear. She hesitated, wondering how to frame a tactful refusal. Then she let out a heavy sigh . . . 'Oh Cynewulf! What happened to us?'

They stood in silent commiseration, as close as they had been for a long time; then Elfrida broke their quiet. 'Are you sure you will be happy with her?' she asked softly. 'You are certain she is the right one for you?'

Cynewulf was positive. 'Oh yes!' he breathed and smiled widely. She makes me feel so good, and manly,' he confided, and they were close again.

Elfrida knew she would be unwise to point out Alicia's many defects. Yet she had to say it. 'Alicia does not like me. She has made that very clear on more than one occasion!'

Cynewulf certainly knew this was fact, because Alicia was not inclined to mince her words where Elfrida was concerned. There were times when he had felt torn between them. 'Is there no chance you could be friends?' he asked hopefully.

Elfrida gave it to him straight. 'We have nothing in common and once you marry her, we part. We will have to!' she explained. It would be even better, if they went to live elsewhere.

'So you'll let me have half of your rents?' Cynewulf persisted. He wanted to buy a new horse, some new clothes for both himself and Alicia, and he wanted new furniture in the

185

matrimonial home. Elfrida was kept by her new father and had no expense at all.

Elfrida wondered if this was the thin edge of some wedge . . . 'Oh very well if Oswald agrees!' she said, covering her back. It stuck in her throat that someone she disliked would profit from her money.

Cynewulf beamed with satisfaction. 'You'll not regret it!' he promised then, having obtained exactly what he wanted, he trotted away to find his sweetheart.

Elfrida felt exasperated with him. She also had a deep sense of foreboding, connected with Alicia, that she could not understand. It ran deep in her psyche, yet was nebulous, leaving her apprehensive for the future.

She shook her head, turned, and trotted off to where the horses were kept. She quickly caught a favourite, mounted and cantered away before giving herself time to think. She simply had to be alone with her muddled thoughts.

She stopped at the entrance to the path and then bent the guardian bush aside. She walked the horse through and rode up to her personal hideout. The cave was as she had last left it and she felt herself relax a little. Once or twice in the summer she had come here, and her horse was used to being led in, a boulder being the marker. She had brought some old skins up and, by tugging another stone to one side, had made herself a fairly comfortable seat on which to sit and muse.

It was an island here. No one knew about it and she considered it her private little kingdom; her personal retreat from the worries of life. Once the bad weather came, she would have to stay away. She could not bear to leave tracks for the sanctuary to be found and used by others.

She let her thoughts run riot over Wulfhere. She was frightened to know she would see him regularly as the weather permitted. She sat quietly, looking over the treetops. Already, many had started to shed their leaves, and she guessed that, on a frosty day when the sun did rise, there would be the most magnificent view towards distant lands.

With a heavy but honest heart, she knew this was her last visit before spring. She flinched at the thought of Cynewulf and Alicia discovering her little secret realm. If Alicia found this cave it would be nothing but a violation because Alicia, she suspected, had not one aesthetic thought in her whole selfish, scheming head.

Just how far did she think she could push Cynewulf? She was always hovering around King Peada with a sycophantic fervent glow in her eyes and she hung on to every word the king said. To Elfrida, it was quite nauseating, and, the trouble was, she was making Cynewulf every bit as bad. Peada too lapped it all up as if this was his regal due.

It floated across her mind to wonder how many other people acted the same way. What would their reaction be when Wulfhere was able to return? She nodded sagely to herself. Burhred was quite right. It was imperative for him to have his ear close to the ground at all times, so he could estimate accurately the people's mood. No matter how she felt, she knew she was the best person to do the distant travelling.

Her heart and her pride were of no consequence. It was a harsh realisation but she was now mature enough to manage. She did make herself a personal vow. When Wulfhere was the new king she would leave. The whole of the country was hers to explore, to travel and roam freely. She was exceedingly well trained and thoroughly self-sufficient, under all circumstances. Oswald would understand, he had been young himself once, but stay in this tun she would not. How could she and see Wulfhere daily?

CHAPTER TWELVE

Wulfhere lovingly polished the sword's blade and admired its make. The hilt had been crafted with loving care and comprised a decorated pattern from numerous twists when the metal had been so hot. It felt good in his hand and gloom hit him because he knew what he had to do without prompting from Aidan.

'I'll go over to take this back,' he said in a hollow voice of dismay, which shouted louder than words.

Aidan smothered a grin. It was going to break Wulfhere's heart to hand the sword back to its rightful owner but he was pleased Wulfhere knew what to do without prompting. 'That's only right and proper,' he replied smoothly. While he was there, he knew the young man would make some excuse or other to see Egwina. What was going to happen in that direction he had no idea and knew he could not stop it anyhow. Events would have to take their natural course, but he was not very pleased. Initially Wulfhere had held the girl in contempt while Aidan had recognised spirit and admired it. Yet, amazingly, they had both swapped places. For some reason, Aidan now felt Egwina to be brittle, even harsh and far more secretive than was good for anyone. Why this should be he had no idea and shrugged. It was totally unimportant. What was more vital was Alcium's return with any message from Burhred. He would, of course, share it with Wulfhere after any necessary censorship.

It was the next afternoon that Alcium came back carrying a small boy on his saddle whom he promptly took over to the large house and his mother. With Wulfhere absent, Alcium was

189

able to give a complete verbal report to Aidan as well as hand over a small, written scroll. After this trip, Alcium almost felt part of some secretive society. He was still very unsure of what exactly was going on, let alone any plans involved, but deep in his heart he was on the side of these enigmatic people. Without the brothers, he and his wife would still be enduring the misery of a very vicious slavery.

'The lady is back?' he asked.

Aidan gave him a startled look. 'No, as a matter of fact, she isn't!' and he felt a twinge of alarm. Surely Burhred would have instructed her to ride directly to him? He chewed his bottom lip with worry but knew there was nothing practical he could do.

Alcium, seeing he was no longer required, hastened to find his beloved Edith, and they fell into each other's arms. Just then Wulfhere and Egwina rode up, beaming at each other, almost as if they had a little secret. The first thing Aidan spotted was the sword. Wulfhere wore it very proudly and Aidan gave him a hard look.

Wulfhere dismounted, then helped Egwina down before he turned to his companion. 'It was given to me!' he hastened to explain, interpreting the glare in Aidan's eyes.

Egwina stood with him. 'It's true!' she confirmed. 'My father said he had won the right to wear it and he didn't wish to fight ever again. He considers himself too old, and such a weapon is fitting for a younger man!'

Aidan was annoyed because it was the weapon of a noble and not a churl. He had a sneaking suspicion that even a direct order regarding discarding the sword would only be complied with reluctantly. He studied the sudden anxiety in Wulfhere's eyes and could almost feel the yearning to have the weapon come from the young man like a wave.

'Very well,' he agreed slowly and had to smother a smile. Wulfhere's expression of worry had been that of a child frightened that a favourite toy would be removed. He did not miss how close Egwina stood to his charge, almost in a proprietorial manner.

He fixed a cold look on his face. 'You have better things to do than be riding around escorting people!' he snapped with bark in his voice.

Wulfhere had the grace to grow pink with embarrassment, and he looked a little helplessly at Egwina. She was astute enough to realise she was definitely not wanted for some reason or other. Wulfhere bent down to give her a quick kiss at the identical moment Elfrida rode into view and watched.

She was immediately upset, but, by willpower, fixed a bland look upon her face as if with total disinterest. Aidan took in the three of them making this scene, frowned at Egwina, glowered at Wulfhere, then turned his unusual testy temper on Elfrida.

'And where do you think you've been?' he grated at her. 'You should have been here first—not last!'

Elfrida was very taken aback and felt her own temper start to flare. 'It's hardly my fault if my horse pulls off a shoe and I have to turn round to go back to get him seen to,' she snapped in her turn. Whatever she had expected to see when next her eyes lit upon Wulfhere it had not been him giving a loving kiss to another female. Her heart had plummeted to somewhere below her stomach, and it took a huge effort to control her emotions into a cold mask.

Aidan was a little taken aback at her terse reply and took time to study her in more detail, which he had never done before. He weighed her up in a flash: open, honest, belligerent when necessary, with a backbone of steel. He made a swift comparison between her and Egwina, and knew who was the better female. He turned and realised Wulfhere was still present, but his attention on Egwina's retreating back.

'What do you think you're doing?' he barked. 'Remove that sword to start with, put it away in the hut, then take that axe and chop enough wood to keep this fire and Alcium's going for a week. Move, I say!'

And Wulfhere did just that. He had learned from experience that when Aidan gave an order in a certain tone of voice it was prudent to obey instantly, to avoid one of Aidan's very large, extremely hard fists.

Aidan watched him move off with alacrity then he turned back to the girl, still sat astride her horse. He stepped forward and looked her straight in the face. 'My apologies,' he said sincerely. 'I'm getting in too much of a habit at barking orders instead of civilised conversation!'

Elfrida gave him a wan smile, dismounted and, as if on cue, Alcium came to take the animal away and attend to it.

Aidan led her into the hut that still had the partition they had erected for Edith. 'You can stay here for the night, but you had better get off first thing in the morning, the weather has started to turn.'

Elfrida gave a huge sigh, quite unable to say what was in her heart. She never wanted to come near here or see the place again, but she had a horrible suspicion Burhred would order her to liaise with Aidan as soon as spring came.

'Now, my dear,' Aidan began with polished manner, offering her drink and food, 'Alcium brought back a brief message from Lord Burhred that all we can do is mark time through the winter. What I'd like you to do is tell me exactly, person-to-person, how things stand, back at the tun.'

So Elfrida told him. Oswald had talked long to her about his worries over Burhred's

193

declining health. She explained the mood of the people, and how the Northumbrian clerks had vanished for the winter. She had to relate that the killer of Eanwulf had never been apprehended. She patiently answered all of Aidan's detailed questions, so he could end up with a perfect political picture.

Then she considered it her turn. 'Wulfhere's training?'

Aidan spoke at length, well aware this information was for Burhred. 'I am very pleased with him, but of course I don't tell him. He wants just a little bit more polish and my job will be done. I will see he works exceptionally hard all through the winter months and I guarantee, by next spring, you will be very impressed with his physique and ability.'

Elfrida itched to ask about the other girl but her pride would not let her. The very fact she said nothing at all told Aidan all he really wanted to know. She was head over heels in love with his young charge who, typically, did not see her. Aidan had no intention of getting himself involved in any kind of complicated love life. His job, his sole brief, was to turn a boy into a man fit to be a king.

Elfrida took herself off early the next day, very anxious now to get away from this area and to return to the security of her home with Oswald. As she rode back, her heart became hard with the determination to leave the area of Mercia as soon as circumstances permitted. With a bit of luck there would only be one more trip to make next spring. Surely after that someone else could take her place as courier? Alcium sprang to mind and she decided he would do nicely. It would not be easy to stand up to Burhred, but she had her own life to lead and she suspected that during a long bitter winter her resolve would become as hard as her heart.

*   *   *

Quite suddenly, the winter closed in over the Hwicce land and it became bitterly cold.

For the first time, both men had felt cold at night. The hot summer had spoiled them. Aidan and Wulfhere worked hard together to insulate their home, as well as that of Alcium and Edith.

The floors were raised a number of inches, well above the soil, and these were thickly strewn with rushes and dried grasses but everyone knew it would not take long for these to become soaked. The wet and cold would arise from the earth and permeate the wooden floors. Draughts would whistle under the door, and through cracks which appeared to be sealed, but could never be made perfect. It would take very little time for their important cooking fire to start off the condensation. It would be just about impossible to wear dry clothes and their sleeping palliases would be equally wet.

Aidan had made plans for his young acolyte. He was confident now Wulfhere was at ease with all the normal weapons of warfare, sword, dagger, axe and spear. He intended to polish him up with all the dirty wrestling tricks he knew. Cyneard's tactic had shown a glaring gap in Wulfhere's martial education.

There was also hunting to do and he planned for Alcium to join in on this. At the back of his mind was the realisation that Alcium of Mercia would make an ideal member of any king's gesith—those vitally important men who were always with the king as bodyguard protectors. A man like Alcium, who had been through so much suffering, but who had emerged as a trusted retainer, was the ideal person to join a royal gesith.

Sometimes, when he looked at Wulfhere, he was frankly astounded at the tremendous spurt of growth that had taken place over these few months: the result of a good, solid, basic diet of meat plus arduous exercise. In his heart of hearts he felt almost smug with satisfaction at what he alone had accomplished.

Deep in his guts he had a feeling that Wulfhere's absence might not be as long as Burhred had initially presumed. The time given to him at the beginning had been two or even three years but Aidan also knew his people. By next spring it was quite possible revolt would begin to fester. Their defeat would be an aggravating sore. Younger men might even be ready to fill the gaps of those who had died near Loidis. In his bones, his instinct, his whole natural being told him to be ready for anything next spring or summer.

Wulfhere continued to thrive on whatever work Aidan threw at him. On a regular basis he begged a precious hour off to ride over to the house to see Ceol. He fooled nobody at all.

There was a totally different atmosphere in the small manor house now that it had been cleaned up, and over which Julie presided like a queen. The horrors of her marriage had been put behind her, and even her children were totally different. They dared to laugh aloud, and to play in a normal manner.

Ceol also welcomed the younger brother called Hoel. He had been touched when his sword had been offered back to him, and it had given him great pleasure to give the young man his first genuine gift. He was under no illusions that he was the real object of these visits, because he understood—boy and girl attracted to each other in youthful loneliness.

He knew nothing at all about the brothers, and they impressed and interested him. They had a story, that was easy to sense, though what it might be he had no idea. He was not overly curious because his experience of life had taught him answers to questions often came suddenly when least expected.

Cuthbert had approached him for his daughter's hand, and he had been glad to approve, but that was another life ago: a past which could never be recaptured from the moment his world had collapsed about him. Now this Hoel, with an unknown background and pedigree, kept turning up on a regular basis, grinning from ear to ear. Once this would have so disturbed him that the young man would have been thrown out. He would certainly like to know more about him, but he was prepared to be patient and wait. All that really mattered was for his daughter to have a new chance to experience happiness.

Ceol also decided that now was the time to look after himself. When his dearly beloved wife had died he had resigned himself to a very lonely old age. This had changed in a flash, because to his absolute amazement, he discovered Julie attracted him.

She was beaten and cowed. She had known nothing but misery in her married life yet, now and again, he fancied he saw a little something display itself. A gentle and soft femininity began to emerge. Even a few timid smiles, and some very tactful questions proved he was only a handful of years her senior. He was charmed with her daughter Ygraine, and that returned boy. At ten and seven years, these children should have been exploding with the joy of life, but they were terrified of their shadows and far too subdued. What an evil man Cyneard had been, and he never ceased to bless the boldness of the two brothers. Whatever their secret might be it was immaterial for the goodness they had done in this little manor house.

So, as the days slipped gently by, he went out of his way to converse with Julie, take little walks with her and pursue a very gentle courtship. He had enormous patience, and the idea of spending the rest of his life with her was most attractive.

With Egwina it was different. She liked Hoel, although she sensed a degree of hostility from the older brother, which was inclined to disconcert her. Her gratitude to both of them was boundless, so charitably, the older brother's terse comments were put down to the fact this blunt speaking was just his way. She did have a problem though, which she had not yet broached to him. It was of huge importance to her and she had no idea of how he thought on the subject.

It was the same regarding him as a person. Who exactly was he? Why this constant effort at polishing, martial skills? After the way he had dealt with the hideous Cyneard she would have considered him perfect. Yet, whenever she came over, he was practising with one weapon or the other, or else he had gone out on long exhausting runs. When he came over to the manor house, ostensibly to chat with her father, she frequently noticed he looked tired—as if his daily physical activities were quite shattering. He always brightened up when he talked to her, although there were times when she fancied he was picking his words with care.

Wulfhere's experience of girls was Spartan. There had been Osburga whom he now realised had been nothing but a tease at his expense. There was the girl Elfrida who acted as courier for Lord Burhred, who seemed to be very standoffish, and this made him rather awe-struck of her. He simply didn't know what to say, nor how to handle her, so obviously she was best avoided. This left Egwina, and he considered her all right. Between Egwina and Elfrida there was nothing at all. They were poles apart.

Egwina had also suffered terribly. Elfrida had not. Egwina was soft and gentle, which appealed to his masculine protectiveness. Elfrida was obviously super-efficient at whatever she did, otherwise Burhred would never use her, let alone want her services. Egwina now had remarkable, almost stunning beauty. Elfrida's looks were simply those of any girl. More to the point, Egwina was here on hand for a peaceful courtship. Elfrida was constantly miles away, and he might never see her again and obviously she had no interest in him, otherwise a male relative or guardian would have sent a message to him.

But he was now very worried because he

had nothing at all with which to plight his troth. Neither did he have anything that could be considered for his Morning Gift, so how could he possibly work around to the delicate subject of matrimony? This seemed an insurmountable obstacle, which taxed his mind each evening before he fell asleep. He had made a firm commitment to himself that Egwina was everything for which he could hope in a wife.

It crossed his mind to wonder what Aidan and Burhred might think about this, yet he considered it a very private matter. Another problem rose regarding his true identity. Half of him said he should disclose all to the female of his choice but the more prudent section warned him to keep his mouth shut still. One man had already been murdered because of him. His instinct warned him he must stay as Hoel until the elder could announce him properly. He was also astute enough to appreciate that if Egwina accepted his suit from Hoel it would show how genuine she was. If he approached as a king in waiting, might she not just come to him for his rank alone? It never entered his head that this thinking was the same used often in the past by the cunning Burhred.

It all came to a head one very frosty day. They both wore thick robes as their feet crunched white frost, which lay so thick it looked like a dusting of snow.

'I want you for my wife, Egwina!' he blurted out suddenly, stopped and took both of her hands in his. 'Will you agree?'

Egwina looked deep into his eyes. She had known this moment had to arrive and felt so sad. Long ago it had been Cuthbert who would say these words, and how willingly she would have agreed. So long dead, which meant he had to be forgotten. She liked Hoel, even with his mystery, and she knew she could not remain single. Besides, she was very much aware of how the wind was blowing between her father and Julie. She was delighted for him, and the fact, probably quite soon, that he would have another wife for company. There was one critical point, though, which she and Hoel had never discussed. Now was the time.

'What is your religion?' she asked quietly.

Wulfhere blinked with surprise. Religion? What did this have to do with marriage? He had always paid lip service to the common gods, especially Woden and Thor. He considered he made his own way in life, with the generous help of people like Aidan, Burhred, Oswald, Ealstan and even Elfrida. 'Why?' he asked, genuinely puzzled. The gods didn't figure in his life really, there was neither time nor space for them.

'I am a fervent Christian!' Egwina replied softly. 'Egwina is not my real name. That was only the name used in my slavery. I have been baptised, and my real name is Mary, and my father's real name is James!'

He stood opened-mouth with amazement. Quite thunderstruck. 'Mary? What a rubbish name! It's not Mercian!' he said with quite a fair amount of disgust.

She looked up at him a little sadly, but with her own degree of firmness. 'No! It is Christian. Not pagan. And from now on I'll only answer to Mary and I would never contemplate matrimony with a heathen, which is what you are, I'm sad to say. When I was a slave, I was raped often by Cyneard and Raebald. It was lucky they did not get me with child—possibly because I was half-starved and ill-treated. I used to pray for release, and you brothers came along and gave it to me, for which I will be forever grateful. But even in the bad, terrible days nothing would have made me forswear my belief in The Christ. I will marry no man who lacks this belief!'

Wulfhere was quite lost for words. He looked into her eyes and was surprised to see how they had gone almost cold and flinty. Christianity? The old, proven gods? What did religion have to do with him preparing to be a king? It flashed through his mind, though, if he really wanted her he would have to come down on her side—and mean it. Sharp instinct warned him this was not a subject for debate. Why! She was another Peada! This realisation gave him a great shock. 'What about your father and Julie?' he said quickly, to gain time.

203

Egwina gave him a smile of pity. 'Didn't you know? Julie has been a Christian for a long time. It was the strength of her religion that kept her sane during her awful marriage to Cyneard,' she explained.

Again, he had not known. Neither had this entered his head. He gave a shrug. 'I would only marry a wife. Not a religion!' he said firmly, and knew he meant it.

She kept equally rigid. If she could not have her beloved Cuthbert she would take Hoel as second best, but never as a pagan.

Wulfhere thought seriously then, and turned aside. King Penda had been a pagan like himself, but also most tolerant of other religions, especially Christianity, as long as no one tried to browbeat him. His brother King Peada was an avowed Christian and a weak pacifist puppet of Northumbria. King Oswiu was a Christian who still made war. He felt initial confusion. Never before had he been up against religious matters, which he considered of no consequence whatsoever. Surely a man's essence was what really mattered?

Then these complicated thoughts were pushed aside temporarily when Egwina spoke again. 'Who are you really? From where do you brothers come? Who are your parents? What is your rank?'

'We are Aidan and Hoel from—' and he waved an arm in a vague circle. 'Aidan teaches! I learn! When he considers my education is

204

complete, I will go forth into the world to make my mark upon it, whatever that might be. Any wife, which I may have, can remain or travel with me, then, one day, when I have seen enough. I will settle down and do exactly what I have to do,' he replied enigmatically. 'People must accept us brothers as we are!' and he had no idea that a bite had entered his voice.

She stared at him fascinated as another mask settled on his face. She hunted through her mind for a word to describe it and it suddenly dawned on her—natural power and position, from past breeding.

He turned back to her. 'And no one, man or woman, will dictate to me how I may or may not worship!' Then without another word, he spun on his heel and walked away, leaving her flat-footed with astonishment and pique.

Wulfhere never turned as he heard her horse ride off at a slow canter. Aidan had been busy in their hut, putting a new edge on his dagger. He was surprised when Wulfhere entered unexpectedly and stood before him, a hard look on his face.

'What's up?' Aidan asked with a flash alarm.

Wulfhere repeated the conversation, just about verbatim, with his excellent memory. Aidan did not interrupt but let him get it all off his chest. Wulfhere paused and stared at the wooden wall for a few seconds, then brought his gaze back to hold his companion's eyes.

'I know I am a king in waiting, taught by the finest trainer in this land, but there is a limit. I will not be dictated to by anyone over a matter that I consider of no consequence in the first place—not compared to the future of Mercia. I could have loved that girl with all my heart and spirit, but I can see now I have made an absolute fool of myself again as I did with Osburga. What kind of marriage would it really have been with the female dictating? None at all! As the son of Penda of Mercia, no female will tell me what to do like that because, at last, I am—a man!' he said, with hot pride.

Aidan carefully studied him, put down the dagger and sharpening stone, and looked into his face. It was amazing. His pupil now topped him in height. His shoulders were even broader. The boy who had come down to be trained here had vanished completely. He would never return. Because here, indeed, stood—a man. The metamorphosis was complete.

Aidan saw his job was done, and, very slowly, with enormous dignity, he bowed his head in salute.

'She wasn't the one for you anyhow. You still can't see what is under your nose, can you?'

Wulfhere blinked. Now what? Then his eyes

206

opened wide with astonishment. 'You don't mean—?'

'Of course I do!'

Wulfhere swallowed. 'But Elfrida doesn't like me,' he protested.

'What do you expect? She rides herself ragged on your behalf and the one time you go for a stroll, you have little to say to her, do you?' Aidan challenged remorselessly. 'You just let yourself be dazzled by that Egwina!' he snapped impatiently.

'She says her name is now Mary!' Wulfhere told him.

'She can get stuffed if she thinks I'm going to pander to her fads and fancies. There are more important matters to hand!' Aidan snapped with some temper. He was not at all sorry this liaison had died its death. Now he would have his pupil's total concentration once more. There was nothing left to teach him; just fitness and muscle power to be maintained. 'Come, let's ride!'

Wulfhere was suddenly glad to get away from the area for a bit, and his spirits rose again as they rode at a fast pace with the cold air making their eyes water. They rode due west, but were finally forced to pull their horses back to a walk. The terrain became unstable to the point of being dangerous, as they approached the mighty River Severn. For a time, they just sat and stared as the water surged inwards on a high tide. The magnificent power of the currents and swirling whirlpools mesmerised them. The river's width and spread was enormous and Wulfhere shivered. No man could survive in that water.

'It's even more dangerous in the spring floods. Over there, across the river in the distant mountains, live the old Celts with another branch of them down in the extreme south-west. They are just about direct descendants of the old British tribes who began to move and migrate after the battle of Deorham, which they lost to the Saxons. They follow all the old customs and make excellent fighters. This river makes a first-class boundary, because very few men have managed to cross it and live. Always know the old boundaries, then you will also know from where your enemies can and cannot come!' he said dryly.

'This is a frightening place!' Wulfhere said as he took it all in, looking around carefully, noting some cliffs further down from them. For a long way behind them lay the wetlands through which they had threaded a track. It was easy to see how often the flood water came this far, because of the various grasses, reeds and general shrubbery.

As they rode back at a more sedate and sensible pace, each was lost in thought. Wulfhere kept going over and over the conversation with Egwina, because, like Aidan, he simply could not think of her as Mary. Now, in the cold raw air, rising in a clinging mist from the river, he knew he had done the right thing. He had to start as he intended to go on by leading from the front and bowing his head to no man or woman. On sober, very cold reflection, he was now honest enough to acknowledge he had been but bewitched by a sheer female presence. Then his thoughts switched to Elfrida—a true Mercian girl who knew all about him, who worked hard for him, who put in many long hours in the saddle to help him reach his goal. Strong, fit and superbly self-sufficient. He also had a sneaking feeling she would make a first-class fighter. He remembered the easy way in which she carried and handled her weapons. When would she come again? Very unlikely before the spring, and then what should he do? If he walked straight up to her and tried to get on friendly terms after just about ignoring her, he would, as like as not, get her hand around his ears. Then the solution hit him. When he returned as king in waiting he would get either Burhred or Oswald on his side. They could speak for him and he would then have a legitimate excuse to start a gentle courtship. Until then, he did not wish to know females, especially Christians!

Aidan's mind moved in a totally different direction. For a little while now, he had felt unease as if a sword was hung above his neck. The cause was quite beyond him, but long ago, he had learned to pay close attention to gut instincts. Something was going to happen in which he would be involved, and he would not like it. By all the gods he had succeeded in his duty, which was all that really mattered.

CHAPTER THIRTEEN

It had been Elfrida's most miserable winter, with the cold going on and on until she felt like screaming with frustration. She felt so cooped up, which did not suit her free roaming temperament. Now and again she ventured outside but even in the tun the snow lay quite deep, and it was a struggle to get about. For the men who had to look after the precious livestock it became a nightmare, and as the bad weather continued for week after week, anxious eyes were cast at the animals' food stocks.

The people did not fare much better, and there were worried comments as the dried meat and grain containers started to empty. One or two of the bolder men had tried to go out and hunt for fresh meat but the game appeared to have vanished, not helped by the proximity of a small wolf pack.

Then mercifully, a wind arose from the west, with an increase in temperature, which brought rain. Everywhere became a quagmire as snow and frost melted in a rush, then, quite suddenly, the rain ceased, the clouds cleared and the sun condescended to reveal itself. With surprising speed, green grass began to show, so, carefully guarded by the younger men, the domestic animals and horses were allowed out to graze. The people followed immediately.

It was vital they find and pick all new buds suddenly showing everywhere. These were hastily eaten, and many taken back to the old and the very young so the dreaded mouth and tooth disease could be stemmed for another year. For some it was too late. Their mouths had swollen and teeth loosened to fall away from swollen red gums. Why the buds and any green food halted this condition, nobody understood. It was old knowledge going back through the generations of humans since the beginning of time itself.

Burhred did not fare at all well. It had certainly been his worst winter and, deep down, he had a suspicion it was his last. Age had waged war on his body, and his pain had been great from the agonies of swollen, red joints. Even with the biggest fire Oswald could safely make in their home, the cold had penetrated everywhere. His biggest problem were red, swollen knee joints. If left too long in one position, they set until it became a fresh agony to move and loosen them.

His mobility suffered in consequence, as did

his temper. It was impossible for him to attend any meetings, and even King Peada was forced to consult his senior elder in his home. The king made numerous solicitous noises, which impressed Burhred not at all.

It was after one of the king's visits that the ugly little idea had entered Burhred's head. He had instantly dismissed it as being far too shaky, but later called it back for more detailed consideration. The more he pondered and weighed up the general situation of Mercia as well as that of his own health, the more he realised it might have merit.

One thing was for certain; it would not be all that long before the Northumbria clerks reappeared to tally the stock losses and to see what tribute Mercia could be reasonably expected to pay in this year.

King Peada was such an innocent it almost hurt Burhred to consider him their ruler. He had shown himself to be even weaker than envisaged. His initial interest in looking after his people had long since evaporated. It was not that he failed to call his council and ask his Witan for their considered advice, it was simply he lacked genuine interest. He seized upon any chance to be closeted with anyone from Northumbria, and King Oswiu. He much preferred to indulge in his passion for verse and ballads.

Burhred knew this was playing right into his hands. He had ordered Elfrida and Oswald to drift out and about among the people, listening to what they had to say. Discreet grumbles were rising, as he had anticipated they would after such a winter. One or two had even begun to criticise their king, because a king's duties were to be seen regularly by the people. He was supposed to hold himself available to head his court and deal with any litigious matters that might arise. He was not expected to spend hours mouthing trite verse, most of which appeared to be Northumbrian in origin.

Burhred passed only one comment, which Oswald and Elfrida understood immediately. 'The fool has started to do my work for me. So be it!'

Oswald and Elfrida exchanged a sharp look, but refrained from comment. Both of them squelched around the mud, listening and returning to Burhred with all they overheard. The only observations that Elfrida kept to herself were those regarding her brother. He had married his Alicia in a blaze of happiness and confidence, but sometimes when she saw him now she thought he wore a hangdog look. She went out of her way to avoid the detestable Alicia because her instinct told her Cynewulf might now be paying for his marriage. She had no intention at all of getting involved in matrimonial upsets. Her brother was a man, and it was time he stood upon his own feet and not come running to her any more—until he was in a position to repay her loan. She had a sneaking suspicion this would take quite a while.

Then Burhred sent her out on a local circuit to pick up the mood of the people from other areas. A female riding alone was sometimes considered unusual except that Elfrida had built herself a reputation for solitariness. Burhred had also cunningly arranged for her to carry small trade goods that the people had made during the winter months: tiny silver brooches of exquisite design, small wooden carvings; items easy to carry in a saddlebag and always popular to trade for coins.

Initially Oswald had been aghast and ready to put his foot down, but a quiet word from his friend and a reassurance of her total self-sufficiency from his adopted daughter had soothed his worry. Oswald could not leave Burhred now, in his crippled condition, and still at the back of his mind at all times was the knowledge that Eanwulf's killer had never been discovered. He did take the precaution of training and giving to Elfrida two large, ferocious hounds. They were guards as well as sentinels.

She rode fully armed with a spear, a shield and two very lethal daggers. She had complete confidence in her ability to deal with all situations. All except one. Wulfhere. Despite mental self-discipline, he never wholly left her mind, and she presumed he had now established a permanent relationship in the Hwicce territory. She could only pray something would happen whereupon Wulfhere could return and claim his right. Once she had seen him do this, she would retire to the little cave to commune with nature for two or three days, then set off on a journey.

*   *   *

Wulfhere was unhappy. He had voluntarily put himself through a rigorous winter training session and knew he had never been so fit and strong. He frequently went out by himself with the full confidence of his trainer. Aidan supervised from long distance, just leaving the hut for necessary tasks. He felt a kind of let-down now his job was done, and he often wondered how long they would have to wait for the call to return; or at least, he added to himself silently, for Wulfhere to go back to fight and claim his rightful inheritance.

Because Aidan knew his own fate. Wulfhere fortunately was blind and he intended for him to stay that way as long as possible. Wulfhere ate alone in the evenings after his day's vigorous exercising because Aidan explained that he ate earlier, enjoying the lovely meals prepared by Edith.

Wulfhere was still somewhat confused. Now and again, he would ride over to see Ceol, as he thought of him, and Julie. It was touching to watch the gentle courtship opening like a spring flower, and sometimes his own heart ached—because Egwina was inflexible to the point of being dogmatic. He had reasoned with himself, attempted the tactics of debate, as Peada would do but Egwina would have none of it. She refused to acknowledge his presence, unless he used her Christian name. Wulfhere had his own streak of stubbornness and simply would not, so their meetings were normally of short duration. Very wisely, her father concentrated on making a new life for himself and refused to be drawn into the young couple's affairs.

Wulfhere simply had no idea that in the girl's eyes he was but a second-best. If it had been destined for Cuthbert to live, the young man called Hoel would not have enjoyed a second glance, let alone be remotely considered. So, very gradually, his visits over to the little manor house began to diminish, and he filled in his spare time with grave reflections on how he would conduct himself when he became king. The Mercian girl courier would intrude upon his mind and, the more he thought about her, the more he swore at himself for letting an obvious opportunity go. As always, he came back to one firm conclusion; that, where females were concerned, he was as ignorant as a babe in arms.

Aidan had a good idea of the direction of

some of his thoughts but no comment passed his lips. He had another more pressing matter to take his attention and as the weeks passed he could only consider one obvious solution. Some days when Wulfhere was out exercising or practising nearby with his weapons, he would stand and admire him before being driven back in to sit on the most comfortable stool. His great fists balled to try to compensate. He was philosophical. He was triumphant at what he alone had done. He was filled with justifiable pride and when the call did come, his product was more than ready. Sometimes he thought, "If only?" then immediately dismissed such base treachery.

It all came to a head one evening when Wulfhere had eaten and the spring sunshine was balmy enough for him to suggest they take their stools outside. Aidan was reluctant but could not think of a good enough excuse to refuse.

Wulfhere sat and surveyed the general scene with quiet contemplation, and immense satisfaction. He had never felt so fit, hard and strong in all his life. He was also filled with supreme confidence, and when he looked back to his old, youthful days he quailed at his memories. He was a different person, another being, and it was all thanks to his brother Aidan who was closer to him than one with a blood tie.

He turned to put some of these thoughts

into words but they died unformed. For the first time in ages he studied his companion and frowned heavily. Aidan had aged! He was deeply shocked at the heavy lines on Aidan's face, then his eyes dropped down and he noted the great hands were in fists, and the forearm muscles were tensed.

'What is it?' he asked in a low concerned voice.

Aidan turned slowly to him. What could he say that would not cause a panic? In many ways Wulfhere was still only a young man, who lacked life's experiences.

'Just a bit off colour!' he managed to get out slowly. 'I'm going back to sit inside. You can admire the scenery for both of us!'

Aidan stood with an effort and forced an artificial grin on his face, which suddenly opened Wulfhere's eyes.

'There is something wrong with you! Are you ill?' and Wulfhere stood so hastily his stool went flying. He reached out to grasp Aidan's upper arm, then froze with the shock. His eyes opened wide as slowly, almost delicately, he ran his hand over his companion's shoulders. Where were the great muscles? They had gone! It dawned upon him that Aidan was but a shadow of himself. He was nothing but skin and bones.

'You are ill!' he gasped with horror. 'There is nothing to you now. By all the gods you are a very sick man! How long have you been like

218

this? What is wrong with you? We must get help—immediately!'

Aidan slowly shook his head. This reaction was that which he had anticipated, and he had given due consideration to the only remedy possible. Now he must placate. 'I'm just a little off colour!' he lied with practised smoothness.

'Rubbish!' Wulfhere said hotly, his face creased with worry and fear. 'I'll get Edith. I'll fetch Julie. I'll get help from somewhere!'

Aidan recognised panic when he heard it. 'You'll do no such thing, because nothing can be done. I am on my way out. There is something growing inside me. Just here,' and Aidan patted his belly. 'You could fetch a dozen healers, and they would be quite helpless. It is something that happens to people, and there is neither remedy nor cure. We all have a time to go and mine is nearly here. You will shortly be on your own, and all I ask is that you do not waste the effort I have poured into your training. And never forget the advice I have given you!'

Wulfhere stood speechless with total horror, then went from one foot to the other. He shook his head violently. 'I won't have it! I will not allow this to happen! Somebody, somewhere must be able to do something. I'll ride back home right away. There must be a healer there who can help!' he shouted.

Aidan took a deep breath, dragged at the last of his strength and shook his head. 'And ruin everything, you fool!' he snarled.

'If you think I wish be to be king at your expense you have underestimated me! I am going for help right now!'

Aidan saw he meant it. He knew there was only one thing to do. While Wulfhere was half-turned, and completely off-balance, he swung his right fist in the last aggressive act he knew he would make. It connected flush. Wulfhere flew backwards and crashed on the ground, out stone-cold. Aidan gritted his teeth, estimated from experience how long he would be unconscious, then turned and forced himself to get a horse.

Wulfhere came to, his wits still bemused. He sat up and shook his head to try and clear it. As memory returned, he staggered to his feet and looked around, still a little bleary-eyed. He was quite alone, and panic hit him again. Aidan could not just vanish.

'Alcium!' he bellowed, and both he and Edith appeared in an alarmed hurry.

'Where is my brother? Do you know?'

Alcium shook his head, quite baffled. Edith then spoke. 'But I saw him ride off only a little while ago. I thought it a bit odd, because he didn't have a saddle. He jumped up on the horse's bare back, lurched a bit over its mane, then straightened up and cantered off!'

'Oh no!' Wulfhere groaned . . . 'What have I done now?'

Alcium stared, deeply puzzled, at a loss as

to what he was expected to do. The younger brother's face wore a haggard look, and he was not quite steady on his feet. Drinking at this hour?

Wulfhere faced him. 'Help me. My brother is ill. I must bring him back and get help!'

Alcium leapt into action. Within a few heartbeats, two horses were saddled and bridled. Once mounted, Wulfhere's instinct was to charge off in a wild gallop but in which direction?

'Circle to pick up his tracks!' he called to Alcium and they parted riding in different directions, then Alcium waved a hand. 'A horse over here, moving fairly fast!'

Wulfhere joined him, studied the muddied hoof prints, raised his head and calculated the direction. 'West! He's heading west!' he cried, and something cold enveloped his heart. He knew exactly where Aidan was heading and his motive. 'Follow me!' he bawled and heeled his horse into a wild gallop. Alcium was taken unawares, then hard put to keep up. It was a crazy pace highly dangerous on slippery ground but Wulfhere never drew rein.

It was not long though, before the earth became too poached, with the horses' hooves slithering in all directions. Alcium let out a huge sigh of relief as they came back to a jolting trot. Wulfhere sat as if carved from stone, eyes staring ahead, face grim. They saw no living creature as they halted on the river's wetland area. Wulfhere studied the earth, desperate to find tracks.

Alcium had only a suspicion what this was about. The iron look on the younger man's face did not encourage one single question. 'A horse has been here, moving to the north!' he shouted and pointed.

Wulfhere joined him, now puzzled as much as anything. Or was it possible that Aidan knew more about this terrain than he had ever let on? They squelched forward, soon liberally splattered with mud, then Wulfhere spotted an object. It was one lone horse, unsaddled, standing rather forlornly with the reins on the earth, one hoof resting on them so the animal had hobbled itself accidentally.

Wulfhere caught his breath. The river was running at what he thought was an ebb tide, and near to the horse was a minute pebble and shell beach not all that far from some red cliffs. He sprang from his saddle and raced over then, eyes down, started to track.

It was simplicity itself. There was little mud at this beach, and only indentations in the sand and some crushed shells showed where a person had stumbled forward to the water's edge. There was nothing else.

Wulfhere stood while a terrible lump grew in his throat and the prickle at the backs of both eyes threatened to burst into a deluge of tears at any second. He scanned the river water anxiously, looking everywhere, but he saw nothing. Just churning currents, some topped with frothy white, and others carrying driftwood down towards the sea. Nothing living showed.

Alcium now understood, and then received one of the biggest shocks of his life. He opened his mouth to speak, knowing what the older brother had done for some reason still beyond him, then he snapped his jaws shut. He caught his breath, while his eyes opened wide with astonishment as he went back, down through the years to when he was a young boy. Suddenly, so much that had puzzled him clicked into place, and he felt humble with this fresh knowledge.

Many years ago, he had been fortunate enough to see King Penda ride through where he lived. Indeed, the king had stopped, leaned out of his saddle and ruffled his hair as he smiled encouragement at a young boy who looked up at him with his child's spear. Alcium had never forgotten. In his mind had been stored a picture of a mighty king.

Wulfhere stood quite unmoving, head up, jaw set, and he had not the slightest idea that, in this particular stance, he was a reincarnation of his dead father. The resemblance was so weirdly uncanny that Alcium lost all speech for a few seconds. Then, very slowly he knew what he had to do, whatever the consequences might be.

He knelt and the movement broke

Wulfhere's concentrated stare at the water. He frowned a little, baffled.

'What do you think you are doing?' he grunted. His mind was half on other matters. The realisation he had lost his brother forever. The knowledge of the secret paper still hidden. The sword, only a noble's weapon. Everything crowded in on him at once, and now this.

'Sir! I know who you really are! You are the son of King Penda, whom I met when a boy. You are the image of him, didn't you know—sir?'

Wulfhere was completely taken aback. This had never entered his head; then he realised it was inevitable his cover would one day be blown. He looked over at the man who faced him, who had bowed respectfully, who had enough knowledge now to arrange for him to be killed. A man who had undergone brutality and cruelty, but who had still managed to live by his personal code of conduct. He knew there was only one thing to do and he knew also Aidan would approve.

'Alcium of Mercia. I am indeed Wulfhere of Mercia, son of King Penda. I am believed to be dead, but I came here to train and to develop but, above all, to wait for the call to return home and collect that which is rightfully mine. I shall gather a gesith about me. Will you do me the honour of being my chief bodyguard, and first member of my gesith?'

Alcium lifted his head and gazed deep into the eyes which held is. 'The honour, sir, is mine. I swear my oath, to serve you all my life!'

Wulfhere managed a thin smile, then held out one hand and lifted his warrior erect again. 'Will you catch that horse, and we will now ride back? Your good lady wife must think we have gone mad, riding off like that. When we do get back will you bring some of Edith's ale and spend the evening with me? Two men alone, because there is much I must now explain to you. Tomorrow I will ride to the manor house, and tell them that my brother is dead. The how and the why. Until then, I would just be very pleased to have your company alone!'

CHAPTER FOURTEEN

Burhred took a deep breath and looked at Oswald and Ealstan. 'Your daughter?' he asked Oswald.

'I did as you asked me. I have sent her out on a small circuit to pick up information. She won't be back for a couple of nights.'

'Excellent!' and Burhred almost purred. 'What I have to say is for you two alone for the time being and when I have explained, you will understand why. The girl can be told some watered-down version, when the moment is appropriate.'

Oswald considered. 'She has become restless. She has told me she wants to leave here and travel this summer. To make a journey. To see life. To meet fresh people!'

Burhred let out one of his famous sniffs. 'She can do what she likes and go where she likes when I have no further use for her. Until then, she is under my orders whether she likes it or not, and the same applies to you as well,' he growled. 'We have all planned and worked too hard for anything to go wrong because of someone's emotions. And let us all remember, there should be another here with us!' he added very coldly.

They all remembered Eanwulf, resented the fact his killer was still free. Oswald and Ealstan looked at Burhred and nodded their agreement, so their senior began to speak to them, taking his time, explaining in great detail his logic.

They were quite alone, the slaves and house servants given some free time, which they had grabbed at eagerly. Oswald pulled a bit of a face at the main proposal.

'That's highly risky for you!' he pointed out soberly.

Burhred flashed his teeth in a combination of grin and snarl. 'As if that worries me at my age, and with my ills. I will not allow myself to go through the misery of another winter like this one has been. No one will be able to touch me, because I won't be here to be touched once I have achieved our goal,' and he turned to Ealstan. 'A few weeks ago some men rode through. You may remember them? They were trading and doing some hunting. They were all foot-loose and fancy-free, idly exploring, looking for a new lord, to whom they could give their oaths and settle down as fighting men. I doubt they will have gone far. I want you to ride after them and give the senior man there a written message from me. It will be short and to the point, without telling them anything more than they have to know at the moment.'

'Which is?' Ealstan wanted to know, highly intrigued.

'That if they hang around, just a little longer, and until our female courier joins them, she will lead them to their next lord!' Burhred stated flatly.

Oswald was all alert. 'I'm not having my daughter's life put at risk!' he said sharply.

Burhred faced him. 'It won't be endangered at all. All I will want her to do is take these men down to Aidan and Wulfhere and escort him back to a given point. Once there, I will ride down to join them and lead our man back to the people. After that, your daughter will have served her purpose and can go on as many journeys as she likes!'

Oswald was forced to admit that this seemed harmless enough, but over the years he had learned just how cunning and savage his friend could be. Over this matter, he was totally ruthless and Oswald could only hope that, in the future, the people of Mercia would know where their debt really lay.

'The people?' Oswald wanted to know.

Burhred nodded. 'Once all the pieces have been slotted into place, and before I haul these old bones on to a horse for the last time, I will speak to them!'

Oswald and Ealstan exchanged looks, which Burhred did not miss. 'It will work if we all play our parts,' he told them firmly.

Oswald could only hope so. He hunted around in his mind for flaws but had to admit there were none to be found as yet. After Eanwulf's unexpected murder though, he could not help but feel a large twinge of unease. There was always the unexpected for which no allowance had been made in the mental equation.

'When?' Oswald wanted to know.

Burhred wasted only a moment, considering. The weather was reasonable. The sun had been shining to dry off the many tracks. The people's grumbles were getting loud enough to disturb the new Northumbrian clerks, who had come down to calculate a fresh inventory for increased tribute. 'Just as soon as your daughter takes it into her head to return!' and he turned to Ealstan. 'As soon as I've spoken to her—alone. I might add—' and he threw a warning look at Oswald '—you get off, find those men and get them eating out of your hand. Take a boy with you so he can come back with a message for me. It needn't be in writing. All I want to know is the day—' and he turned back to Oswald '—then you can get me mounted. I will warn the people, then go and meet our new king!' he said confidently.

Oswald cleared his throat. 'He won't walk into the position like Peada did. He'll have to fight,' he warned soberly.

Burhred threw him a wolfish leer. 'After what Aidan's told me of his progress there won't be a man around able to touch him!'

'I just hope you're not being too sanguine,' Oswald added to himself but had sense enough to keep this pessimistic observation to himself. He will also deeply concerned about Burhred's ability to sit upon a horse, let alone ride one even at a walk. He ran his mind's eye over the animals available and mentally selected one that was known to be absolutely quiet. He also resolved to ride with his friend to catch him if he should look like falling off. It was all an immense worry to him, and he just wished the days would fly by so their situation could be resolved one way or the other.

Elfrida returned exactly four days later to find the whole place was in turmoil with people gathered in little groups of twos and threes, talking in a hushed tones, all obviously deeply shocked. She dismounted, removed her saddlebags, which had many coins from successful trading, and started to walk to her home the back way. She did not feel like indulging in talk or gossip of any kind. She just wanted to see Oswald, change her clothes, get the slaves to bring some hot water so she could feel clean again from hair to foot. She also felt a deep weariness in her bones. She yearned to get away and explore the big wide world. Quite suddenly, all this business, and the subterfuges of king-making had palled.

It was unfortunate that also coming round the back way was her brother. 'Elfrida!' he gasped and hurried over to her, grabbing one arm. 'Isn't it terrible?'

Elfrida looked at him wearily. His eyes were aglow with some type of shock, yet also on his face there were fresh lines. He looked as haggard as if he were ten years older. So much for marriage to Alicia, she thought. It looks as if the rot has set in there. 'What is it? I've only just returned from trading, and I am very tired,' she said firmly.

'But it's the king!' he cried.

'Well what about Peada?' she asked resignedly. It was obvious he wouldn't go away until he had given her some news.

'He's dead!'

Elfrida was thunderstruck, quite speechless for the moment then her wits moved into action. A warning was sounded in her mind, and she caught her breath. Lord Burhred! He would want her for something or other, and her heart sank like a heavy rock.

'You are quite sure? How?' she managed to get out, stunned with disbelief.

'Nobody knows yet. He was found dead in bed this morning. The Witan is meeting, but everyone is still in shock so nothing can take place for two or three days at least!'

Elfrida shook her head and pushed him aside rather rudely. 'I'm too tired to bother. I'm off home!' she told him firmly, then strode on while her mind buzzed with this information.

Burhred spotted her coming, turned to Ealstan and nodded. 'Get off as quickly you can. I'll see the girl catches you up in the morning.'

The first person Elfrida saw as she stepped into her home was Burhred, and she could not help but flinch at the implacable look on his face. He read her mind as easily as always, and spoken first.

'Yes, I know you're tired out. I know you're fed up but this is the last time I shall want your help. It is not for me but for Mercia. I want you to leave at the dawn and ride down to liaise with Ealstan who will have four men with him,' and he explained the meeting place. 'You will then take the five of them down to collect Wulfhere and Aidan. The time has now come!' and he paused again, his tone triumphant.

'Once you have done this, the last service for me, you can do what you like, and go where you like, though I thought perhaps you might like to see Wulfhere come into his own?'

Elfrida made herself consider that and gave a brief nod. She opened her mouth to pass a few pertinent comments but Burhred again forestalled her.

'I have worked out the times very carefully. In exactly two days at noon I will be at the spot where you originally pick up the men and Ealstan. I will then lead Wulfhere back home. I think I have earned the right, don't you?'

Elfrida nodded and gave him a weak smile. 'You certainly have!'

'Before I leave here to collect our next king, I will speak to the people and warn them what is going to happen,' he explained to her.

Elfrida had to chuckle then. It was all quite brilliantly planned, not that she ever expected anything else from this devious, cunning man. But she could not resist a dig. 'Are you sure you're able to get on a horse, let alone ride one?'

'Don't be impertinent! You're not too important to avoid having your ears boxed!' he shot back at her but he was quite amused at the spirit, which could still produce cheek even when exhausted.

'I shall then go on a journey after I have spent a couple of nights in a cave I found where I can just commune with myself,' she told him in a low voice.

He nodded sagely. 'I wondered if you had discovered it and used as a retreat. I often went there myself as a young man to sort out my problems and if you have a skill at tracking, which I know you do have, you've realised that's where Wulfhere hid until Aidan collected him. Don't let people know about this retreat. It's almost too sacred for everyone to know and use,' and now he spoke more to himself than to her.

They looked at each other. Age and youth bound together in one dangerous project, and, for the very first time, there was mutual rapport between them, considerable respect and solid friendship. Instinctively, Elfrida stepped forward and kissed one weather-beaten, leathery cheek. As she turned to go to her cubicle she was amused to see the elder had blushed scarlet.

*   *   *

In the afternoon of the very next day, Elfrida led the way with Ealstan and four very hard-bitten warriors following her. It had all gone off with great simplicity. It had been a short ride to find the little gathering, where Ealstan had vouched for her and the men had been quite happy to fall behind her lead. She was conscious she was the focus of all their attention and they even deferred to her with considerable respect. That she had been doing something quite remarkable had never entered her head, and she felt a little embarrassed at the attention they gave her.

They threaded their way through the last of the trees into the open space of the little manor house and approached at the identical moment Wulfhere and Alcium also rode up. The two little groups looked at each other with considerable surprise. The warriors behind Elfrida broke into a barrage of low conversation among themselves.

Even Elfrida was forced to catch her breath with astonishment. This was not Wulfhere. This was—King Penda! This was not the erratic youth she had known and fancied. This was a hard-bitten adult male, who carried himself as if a king already.

Elfrida turned in the saddle, lifted a hand to halt her retinue so she could ride forward to Wulfhere alone.

He was equally flabbergasted as his attention riveted on the girl, and he knew instantly that this was the one for him, but would she even look at him after the past? He was at a total loss for words, then her horse was against his.

'The time has come, Wulfhere of Mercia. Our Lord Burhred will be waiting for you not all that far away to escort you to your people. King Peada is dead!'

'What?'

'And Aidan is also wanted,' Elfrida told him.
'He's dead too. Yesterday!'

They looked at each other, both stunned into temporary silence, while they hastened to digest this double revelation.

'What happened?' they asked simultaneously.

Elfrida was the first to collect her wits. 'I think we both have a lot of explaining to do to each other—here and now is neither the time nor the place.'

Wulfhere nodded slowly and became aware they had a little audience from the manor house comprising Ceol, Julie and Egwina with the servants and slaves. Visitors were so rare that everyone automatically turned out to find out what was going on.

Everyone was looking at everybody else, when the most piercing scream cracked through the air, startling all of them. All eyes became riveted upon Egwina who dashed before them all straight to one particular warrior.

'Cuthbert!' she cried, tears suddenly streaming down her cheeks. 'I thought you were dead!'

The warrior almost fell from his horse in his haste to dismount, then, settling his balance, he spun on his heels, grabbed the shocked girl to him and plastered her with kisses. 'I thought you were too! Oh my sweet darling!'

Everyone watched in total amazement, then

Ceol stepped forward. He grasped Cuthbert's hand but could only stand holding it, too choked for speech. Then Egwina controlled herself because she knew what she had to say, even if it damned her in his eyes.

'I am not as I was in the past,' and she lowered her eyes unhappily. 'I am no longer a maiden. I have been raped repeatedly by two men,' and she waited holding her breath with anxiety.

Cuthbert's face filled with blood, and his face became an ugly mask, as her words registered. 'You are still mine. That was not your fault. Point out the two men to me!' he demanded in an outraged voice.

Egwina hastened to explain. 'They're both dead. Hoel killed them for me, and he and his brother released us from slavery.'

Cuthbert looked to where she pointed. 'Hoel?' he asked blankly. 'That's the man we've come to serve, if he will take our oaths when he becomes king. That's Wulfhere of Mercia. Son of King Penda!'

Now every eye switched direction, but Wulfhere sat erect in his saddle then, with a dignity which would have made Aidan proud, he bowed his head to them all.

'My people,' he began, his gaze sweeping over them all in turn, remembering how his father had mesmerised a gathering. 'I am on my way back to fight and claim my rightful inheritance. My brother died yesterday and I

236

am sad he will not be at my side, because, if I am fit to be king, it is he who has made me so. This splendid female courier has much owed to her by myself and Mercia as a whole. To you people who live here, once I am king and I will let you know, all this land, known as Hwicce tribute land, and this manor is given rent- and tribute-free. I will see a clerk comes down with the appropriate documentation. In the meantime, let someone ride with me, as your messenger so you will always have up-to-date news.'

There was a thunderstruck silence, then a ripple of applause, which grew in volume. Feeling more than a little embarrassed at his very first public speech, Wulfhere flashed a look at Ealstan and Cuthbert, then pushed his horse forward for the return journey to his destiny.

Elfrida was lost for words. She had expected nothing like this, and, with a nod at Wulfhere, she moved into the lead, then cantered off in the van to put Burhred in the complete picture. She rode automatically, mesmerised with everything she had seen and heard.

*   *   *

She arrived back home first to a tun that was buzzing with rumour, gossip and highly excited speculation. After passing her horse to be attended to, she walked through the crowd,

237

taking in various comments.

'They said he was killed out hunting!'

'That elder is too cunning for his own good!'

'But who killed King Peada and why?'

'Wulfhere will be no good. He was an arrogant brat!'

'Yes, we want a proper man. Not the likes of him!'

'I'll challenge him!'

'Me too!'

She reached her home, an empty place at this minute, then Cynewulf appeared. 'Sis! Alicia wants me to challenge for the right to be king!' he blurted out.

She would, Elfrida thought with exasperation. 'In which case I'll be arranging your funeral,' she warned him soberly. 'Oh brother. Look at you! I've never seen you so miserable. It was a mistake, wasn't it? For goodness sake, divorce her!' she advised.

'I wish I could but I can't afford the settlement. I've spent all my money on clothes and things!' Cynewulf blurted miserably.

Elfrida gave him a very stern look. 'Don't ask, because the answer is no!' she said coldly. 'Now go away and leave me alone. I want to have a gentle walk and use muscles not connected with the saddle, and no, you can't come with me either! Go on! Scat!' she said briskly and strolled away.

Cynewulf watched her depart miserably. He was in an awful mess and knew it. The only person who could really help him was his sister. He bit his bottom lip thoughtfully, then making himself move very silently, he padded after her. If he waited a bit, she might change her mind and help him.

Elfrida for once, had no idea at all that someone was on her trail. She was just deeply engrossed in all that she had seen during the last days. Wulfhere had changed so much. She wondered how she had ever dared to fancy him. Now he was already remote.

She walked on towards the weapons' practice ground, guessing it would be empty when there was so much of an uproar going on. As she approached, though, she heard the particular thud caused by a spear hitting a tree. Parting some shrubs, she peeped through and was astounded to see it was Alicia. As she spied, Alicia picked up a second spear, and with a very fluid movement threw again. It was so accurate the spear's metal point landed in the direct spot of the first and dislodged it. Then in the twinkling of an eye she picked up her third spear, and threw this. It was a quite astonishing exhibition of the art of throwing the spear, so that three weapons landed in the identical spot, each dislodging the other.

Elfrida was stunned. She had never realised Alicia could even handle a spear, let alone with such expertise. Then it hit her and she caught her breath. She waited until there were no weapons to hand, then jumped into the clearing, giving Alicia a shock.

'You killed Eanwulf!' she accused.

Alicia faced her, saw she was alone, then pulled out her own dagger. 'So what if I did?' she snarled like a treed wild cat.

'But why?' Elfrida cried. 'What had he ever done to you?'

Alicia slowly advanced, dagger in her right hand. 'I thought it was that senile Burhred! He's always all over you and he is against Northumbria when our future is there with them. I think he is at the back of King Peada's death and intend to say so!'

'I think you are—mad!'

Alicia wasted no more energy on words. She advanced a half circle and Elfrida immediately had her own dagger ready so that it was held correctly with the blade pointing upwards for the gutting cut.

Elfrida felt ice-cool and collected. She had rigid control of her mind and had blanked everything from it except the need to survive. Alicia tried a couple of stabs as feints and Elfrida parried with her own blade. Each pushed against the other, estimating the strength in the arms, then Alicia moved very fast. Elfrida sidestepped, then in a movement she had practised so often in the past, she switched her dagger from her right to left and plunged it upwards. Alicia was taken completely by surprise and had no chance at all. Elfrida's dagger sank into her middle,

240

travelling very fast upwards, fatally rupturing the great aortic artery. Elfrida jumped backwards as the blood gushed out in a fountain, while Alicia stared with total disbelief.

'You've killed me!' she managed to croak, as her body starting draining.

'As you killed Eanwulf!' Elfrida said, then watched solemnly as Alicia's body slumped to already blood-soaked soil.

Cynewulf stepped into the clearing, making his sister jump with shock. 'I heard it all. I saw it all. She was going to kill you, like Eanwulf!' he said slowly, and shook his head with disbelief. 'I never realised I was married to a murderess!'

Elfrida eyed him sharply. He did not have her strength, and she knew she must do something immediately before her brother passed out looking at the enormous pool of blood.

'Quick! Go back to the tun. Bring help back. Hurry!' she shouted at him.

He was galvanised into action by the tone of her voice, by what he had witnessed and by the awful knowledge he had been married to an evil female. He spun on his heels and bolted, running in manic fashion, bouncing off shrubs and trees. He burst into the centre of the tun where Wulfhere sat on his horse, his retinue at his rear and Burhred, Oswald at his side, ready to address and reintroduce a son of King

Penda to a huge crowd.

Cynewulf burst forward, charged through the crowd of people, sending many stumbling, as wild-eyed with his shock, he reached Lord Burhred. They were all taken aback at this frantic intrusion, and Cynewulf grabbed the first mounted leg, holding onto it frantically.

'Quick! Help!' he garbled wildly. 'It's my sister!' he howled frantically. 'She's just had a fight with Lord Eanwulf's murderer and killed her!'

Wulfhere blinked. Whatever he had expected when he returned it was certainly not this. Was it a madman holding his leg in such a savage grip? It was Burhred who recovered his wits first. 'Where?' he barked while the crowd fidgeted with its own shock.

'The weapons' practice ground,' Cynewulf managed to blurt out.

Oswald stood in his stirrups, then eyed Wulfhere. 'Good people! Let me through! Business calls!' Wulfhere cried and taking their cue from his calm manner they moved aside to give him passage. With Cynewulf stumbling ahead, very unsteady on his legs now, they followed him the short distance to the weapons' practice area.

Elfrida stood exactly where her brother had left her, the body near her feet, where there was a huge pool of blood. She was in control of herself but, even then, totally unprepared for the horde of people who arrived led by

Wulfhere with Burhred slightly to one side watched by an anxious Oswald.

Wulfhere dismounted, and Cuthbert and Alcium copied, to move at his side protectively. Wulfhere was astounded and he took in the scene. Elfrida faced him, her dagger still in her hand but the point downwards now, her arm and hand relaxed. Those who could get near enough to see turned and rumbled their observations to the ones behind.

'What happened exactly?' Wulfhere asked quietly. It was that girl again!

Elfrida calmly told her story. She did not omit a word, nor exaggerate. 'Unknown to me, my brother was hiding nearby and witnessed it all!' she finished simply.

Wulfhere turned to Cynewulf who was in a state of shock and disbelief. He told his story, but it was disjointed, though Wulfhere did not hurry him. Burhred said nothing. He was interested in how Wulfhere conducted himself and handled the situation in general.

'Very well,' Wulfhere said finally. 'One of you remove the body to somewhere satisfactory, and then you and you—' pointing to the brother and sister '—will come before the Witan and repeat your story and answer any questions that may be put to you!'

Burhred nodded with complete satisfaction. He could not have handled the situation better himself and he smiled warmly at Oswald and

Ealstan. It had all been a huge gamble from start to finish, but events today were proving enormously satisfying. Mercia would not go far wrong now, and, turning slightly, he sought two Northumbrian clerks, and with great pleasure and not a little malice, he glowered at them. 'Your days are very numbered now!' his hard eyes told them and they broke eye contact first in worry and despair.

CHAPTER FIFTEEN

Wulfhere stood almost casually in the square and, around a well-defined perimeter, the people huddled in tightly packed ranks. He smiled quietly to himself, fully aware that Aidan still hovered somewhere near his right shoulder. This . . . was it.

He turned and threw a grin at Alcium who stood proudly behind him, flanked by an ever-grateful Cuthbert. The other warriors huddled near, wondering who might be invited into the gesith. It was such an honour. Slightly to one side sat that enigmatic girl and, beside her, her huge brother. Oswald had already given him a brief run-down of people and Cynewulf interested him. A king's gesith had to be balanced. It required men with brains, who were obedient and trustworthy and also, at times, a pure muscle man for when brains did not count—someone of immense strength—and Cynewulf of Mercia fitted into this latter category easily.

The people talked amongst themselves as Wulfhere walked around calmly, in complete control, quietly enjoying himself. He spotted the mystery girl, as he thought of her, and he knew he would have to do something immediately after this fight. He was deeply relieved that Eanwulf's killer had been dealt with, and also shocked to learn the murderer had been female.

Burhred stood up and caught everyone's attention. 'Silence!' he bellowed. 'The first challenger is Merefin!'

Wulfhere went on high alert and rapidly assessed the opposition, who marched up to him. Names which began with an M were unusual and not normally Mercian. He viewed a man in his late twenties with a grizzled face, not over tall but powerfully built on square lines—a man of experience.

'Weapons?' Wulfhere asked politely.

'Sword and dagger!' Merefin requested, he too eyeing up his opposition. Facing him was youth and fitness but, he guessed, little battle experience if any at all.

Each man took his weapons from a common stockpile, in which they were all the same. Wulfhere opened first, his sword blade dancing to right and left as he advanced remorselessly. Merefin was completely taken aback. He had

245

been prepared for the normal half-circling, while looking for a killing opening. This constant advance was something totally new, and he reeled backwards, moving flat-footed, so he would not stumble. He tried a few stabbing blows of his own, then was forced back onto the defence.

Suddenly, and the challenger never quite knew how it happened, his opponent's sword tip had shot neatly through the hilt guard, when, with an adroit twist, his wrist and hand were twisted upwards and outwards, and his sword flew from its hand. Before he had time to swing up his dagger, his sword had gone flying through the air. The next heartbeat Wulfhere's sword tip rested against the great artery in his neck.

'Yield?' Wulfhere grated.

Merefin was totally taken aback at the speed with which he had been dismissed. 'I yield!' he gasped, bleakly horrified at such a defeat.

'Will you swear your oath to me?' Wulfhere asked in a voice loud enough for everyone to hear.

'I swear, my lord!' and Merefin meant it with respect.

Wulfhere lowered his sword, gave the man a grin, slapped him on the back and gently pushed him back to the crowd. 'Next!' he bawled.

The people burst into talking, marvelling at

what they had just witnessed. Sympathetic eyes rested on Merefin whose forearms streaked blood.

Wulfhere threw a look at Alcium with whom he had already discussed a certain subject and received a swift nod.

Wulfhere now strode over to where Merefin was attending to staunch the blood loss, with the end of his tunic.

'Merefin, that man there—' and he pointed at Alcium '—heads my gesith. Would you like to join him?'

Merefin blinked with genuine surprise. He had been in many such fights, but never before had such a position been offered to him. He became aware that every eye was now fixed on him and he reddened with pleased embarrassment. 'The honour would indeed be mine, sir!'

'Then get over and join Alcium!' Wulfhere told him generously.

The people approved with vociferous cries, and a few handclaps. How different was this son of Penda to the luckless, effete Peada. This one was to their taste and approval. Such speed and skill with weapons! What incredible fitness and strength! Mercia would do no better elsewhere.

'I challenge!' another called, and pushed his way forward. There was a general subdued snigger from the people and Wulfhere had to hide a smile. This one was either a supreme optimist, or had a big opinion of himself. It then occurred to him the real reason was the thought that he too might be invited to join the gesith. There was even a line of fat pushing over the waistband of his trousers.

'Weapons?' Wulfhere invited again.

'Just the axe!' was the reply.

Burhred was also taken aback. This man was just about past doing anything except sitting round the campfire, drinking ale and telling stories. It was a total farce but provided entertainment for the people who would talk about this for long afterwards.

The axeman came forward, swinging his weapon, telegraphing every move he intended to make so Wulfhere suddenly dropped his axe and ducked under that which was descending on him. He used one of Aidan's superb wrestling moves. He spun around, hips to hips, and threw the man neatly. He followed this up by straddling him and pressing his large hands around a rather fat neck.

'Yield?' Wulfhere asked, then decided to play to his fascinated audience. He rolled his eyes in mock disbelief and shrugged at his people. They burst into a barrage of hooting laughter and jeering comments as the man on the ground struggled to catch his breath in his anxiety to cede.

As Wulfhere stood he dragged the man up with him, spun him around then, sensing the people's need, he planted a hefty kick on his backside. The crowd roared its approval and simultaneously, moving as one and as if planned, they surged forward to crowd around him, slap his back, touch him, then two stalwarts bent and lifted him onto their joint shoulders.

'King Wulfhere!' they chanted enthusiastically.

'We have ourselves a new king!'

'It's Penda come back to us!'

'Long live Mercia!'

They paraded him around while Wulfhere beamed from ear to ear. Never had he dreamed he would be so feted and the one great sadness that filled his heart was the absence of his much loved and cherished brother Aidan.

Burhred decided it was high time he controlled the situation. He limped forward, nodded with approval, then picked up one of Wulfhere's arms before fixing his gaze on the elders.

'I said I would give you a king. A real king like old King Penda. Do you all accept him?'

The roar of assent that rose from every mouth, except those of the Northumbrian clerks, was loud enough to make some nearby horses fidget with alarm. Wulfhere looked all round, seeking her, but she had vanished! What he did see were the hostile clerks. He scrambled down from his human carriers and pushed through the people. He strode over to them and gave them both a hard glare.

'If you want to stay healthy—get from my land!' he growled.

The unfortunate clerks looked at each other with alarm, then turned to push a path through the people to their horses. Their ears rang with catcalls of mockery, and they were roughly manhandled by Mercians who now knew they had come into their own again, at long last.

Wulfhere watched them go, even managing to feel a tiny bit sorry for them, and suddenly Burhred was by his side.

'No! Say nothing. I did it for Mercia—not you!' the old man grated. He felt tired to the marrow of his bones and also glowed with the most immense, internal satisfaction that his complicated plans had come to this splendid fruition.

'I can't see her!' Wulfhere exclaimed. 'I must! Where would she be?'

A twinkle appeared in Burhred's old eyes. 'Think!' he rebuked gently.

Wulfhere frowned uncertainly, then had his own revelation. 'The cave!' he gasped in a low voice.

Burhred grinned and gave a tiny nod. He wanted to go home. He wanted to sit on his favourite stool with a good ale and Oswald to keep him company. His work was well and truly done, and his old body told him he did not have all that much longer to go. He did not mind in the least. As everything has a beginning, so must it also have an ending.

Wulfhere whipped around. 'Alcium, get horses!' he roared. 'Cuthbert, you men—I make you my gesith. Let's ride! I'll take your personal oaths later before the Witan!'

With a burst of alacrity, excitement, and wild enthusiasm, King Wulfhere of Mercia vaulted onto his horse and thundered along a well-remembered path with his new gesith at his heels.

Elfrida had left her horse with long hobbles so he could graze in comfort. She sat at the mouth of her cave, thinking deeply of all that which had happened. Now she was—free to pursue her own life. Her heart soared although the happiness was muted. She had the shock of her life at the approaching noise because many hoof beats moving at a gallop, make their own brand of thunder. She swore with anger. What was Cynewulf up to now? How dare he follow her here! Her face set like granite and her jaw dropped as King Wulfhere burst into sight, coming up the path very fast.

'There you are!' Wulfhere cried with relief. 'I want words with you!'

The king jumped from his horse while Alcium caught the reins and dismounted more slowly. Cuthbert joined him while the remainder of the men followed suit, then crowded near the cave entrance. Wulfhere grabbed Elfrida's arm and hauled her into the privacy of the cave.

'What is it?'

'What's going on?'

'Does he fancy her?'

'Can you hear what they are saying?'

'Shut up so we can listen!'

The men stood straining their ears but not a sound reached them to their mutual frustration.

'It's too quiet!' one commented.

'Now he's caught her, he's having it off!' suggested another.

After what seemed an interminable time, Wulfhere and Elfrida walked into view. Eyes carefully scanned their attire.

'I bet he did! He's had the time!'

'What do you bet?'

Wulfhere and Elfrida exchanged amused looks, perfectly well aware they were the object of ribald comments.

'Come on, we will go home together,' Wulfhere told her gently, holding her hand.

As they walked past the men who lined up respectfully on two sides, she leered at them, highly amused. 'I'm not telling, so you'll never know!' she teased.

Wulfhere wore his own grin. 'I second that comment too!'

It is very difficult to research the Dark Ages. The works available are Bede's writing; the *Anglo-Saxon Chronicle*; the *Historia Brittonum* and some odd letters from the religious. The snag is they do not all agree and there is a degree of romanticism present.

Certain facts are agreed though. Wulfhere was hidden by three earldormen. King Peada was murdered by poison and his wife suspected. No explanations are given.

Elfrida did not marry Wulfhere and there are many reasons. Marrying for love was just about unheard of. Marriage was for political alliances and like only ever married like. Although well bred, Elfrida was neither royal nor noble.

Now, with her work done, she was free to roam and explore with or without her new father. She would realise she had been but obsessed with Wulfhere and the new king had only one true thought on his mind: to thrash Northumbria.

This he did. Wulfhere acquired his army, marched on King Oswiu and defeated him, so freeing Mercia from the yoke of being a tribute tribe. King Oswiu then retired to a religious life.

Wulfhere's queen came from Kent. He was pagan but turned to Christianity, though in a rather half-hearted way.

Wulfhere went from strength to strength, consolidating Mercia's position until he became overlord of the bulk of southern England. He reigned for seventeen very good years though this ended in disaster again versus Northumbria. He died in 675, thought to be from disease.

As to the man himself: he soon reverted to paganism. It is during this period he is thought to have killed two of his own sons who had become ardent Christians. When Wulfhere found out, he flew into an uncontrollable rage and slaughtered them both. After this he was filled with remorse and subsequently became a sincere and genuine Christian. To make some atonement for his sons' deaths he completed the construction of a monastery begun by Peada. This is thought to be somewhere in the region of today's Peterborough.